True North

Also by André Mangeot

POETRY
Natural Causes (Shoestring, 2003)
Mixer (Egg Box, 2005)

FICTION
A Little Javanese (Salt, 2008)

True North

ANDRÉ MANGEOT

SALT

CAMBRIDGE

PUBLISHED BY SALT PUBLISHING
14a High Street, Fulbourn, Cambridge CB21 5DH United Kingdom

© André Mangeot, 2010

The right of André Mangeot to be identified as the author of this
work has been asserted by him in accordance with Section 77
of the Copyright, Designs and Patents Act 1988.

Printed in the UK by the MPG Books Group

Typeset in Bembo 12 / 13.5

ISBN 978 1 84471 828 3 paperback

1 3 5 7 9 8 6 4 2

For Dan Griffiths & Dennis Burden—

great teachers both, with fondness and thanks

Over the centuries civilization has been carried by various powers: myth, religion, metaphysics. Although remnants of all these remain, usually in degraded forms, today civilization is carried by nothing — it just grows and spreads, like a cancer.

KENNETH WHITE — *The Wanderer and his Charts*

Contents

Rain

H e ' d s p e n t t h e morning deep in the Carpathian forests, feeling like a god. The air was pure, so clear it felt eternal; and this was his kingdom.

Radu, his guide from the sawmill, might have read his mind.

'See — straight to heaven!' he called across the clearing, slapping his palm against a ninety-foot pine. Another perfect column, soaring out of sight in their mountainside cathedral. Shafts of sunlight arrowed back from the canopy as if through stained glass. Lucas scuffed at the soft floor of needles with his boot, watched the dust-motes dancing with colour.

He'd asked Radu to bring him up here, past Magiresti, to see for himself the extent of McAllister's holding.

'There — the white hills,' Radu pointed. Over the Tazlau river, far below. Up across the valley to distant ridges of beech, oak, spruce, silver fir. A vivid necklace — gleaming facets of green, copper, gold — circling the peaks still frosted with snow.

'*All* of it? Are you sure?'

He'd seen photos, memorised the map, but out here the sheer scale — trees, ravines, mountains — was astounding.

'Of course,' Radu answered, checking his watch. 'Come, is time we go back.'

Lucas had rarely felt so alive. Everything held an

electric clarity. Some trip, he reflected, inhaling the rarified air. The best trip ever.

The concept of delegation had always been alien to his father. Still, it was clear to Lucas that thirty-four years at the helm had, increasingly, played tricks with John McAllister's reason. Had nurtured, through lack of challenge, a sense of inviolability; the illusion that he alone *was* the company, indispensable to its success.

No one could dispute his father's capacity for work, his utter dedication to the business. Without his vision, energy and self-belief the modest joinery business he'd inherited from *his* father, John senior, would never have flourished as it had.

Growing up, Lucas and his mother saw little of him as a result. He was always *abroad* or *in the City*. (As a child Lucas imagined this must be Nottingham, just up the road and the only city he knew). His father was off raising funds, along with his profile. On the scent of ailing rivals, vulnerable balance-sheets. In time Lucas came to resent even his brief appearances, the token attempts at bonding. Painful hours repairing a bicycle tyre; barked reprimands at another failed tackle; fending off leg-breaks bowled through a low and blinding sun—these were just a stranger's intrusion into self-imagined worlds he already much preferred.

Little wonder, then, that 'succession planning' was something his father resisted, avoided speaking of, for as long as possible. Partly down to arrogance, but also because Lucas showed no inclination to follow him. And since there was no clear alternative, the status quo prevailed. Approaching seventy but still in rude health, the boss soldiered on. Expansion continued apace. McAllister acquired further forests, mills, timber yards. The numbers not only made sense, they were startling. Investors liked what they saw. Profits soared.

Lucas, now a young man, pursued different paths, dreams, girls. None, in his father's eyes, were suitable—but that was largely the point. At fourteen, a junior squash champion and talented cricketer too, Lucas had toyed with the idea of professional sport. By seventeen though, it had all gone to pot—quite literally. After several warnings, suspensions and plummeting grades he and two friends were finally expelled from their West Country boarding school for dealing dope to fellow Sixth Formers. Lucas had stumbled on the enterprise by chance in the local pub, where he and other final-year students were allowed for a weekend pint. The swift conversion of product into cash (which funded the best CD collection in school) was too simple to ignore.

His mother—forever supportive in the wake of each paternal blast meted out on her son—did her best to rescue something positive. At one point, bless her, Lucas recalled her suggesting that he'd 'at least displayed initiative,' a budding if misguided flair. But this cut no ice with her husband. One swift telephone call to an ex-army colleague in Skye was enough to banish Lucas into exile with the clear imperative: here the party ends. *Time to examine yourself, sonny. Where you are heading.*

Major Savage more than lived up to his name. His daily regime was draconian: a lung- and back-breaking mix of assault course, peat-cutting and unrelenting discipline. Shape up or ship out. Within a week, lying in the bleak little croft, aching head-to-toe from his latest exertions as the wind moaned outside, Lucas's mind was, indeed, fully focused.

It was there that it came to him — what his rebellion, such as it was, was about. If he wanted to accumulate anything it was experience, not wealth. Money, above all, had nurtured the distance between him and his father. Not simply the time it took to make it, its costs and demands, but the money itself. Doled out more in apology, a substitute for warmth or embrace. Understanding this, Lucas underwent a strange but sincere transformation. Realised it was how one approached things — one's own state of mind, not the thing itself — that mattered. Much to his own astonishment he awoke the next morning resolved to make a go of it. Father and son. Learning the trade. He saw now that experience was everywhere, including McAllister's. The rest was what you made of it.

It took close to six months for his father to believe in the change, to entrust him with anything approaching a meaningful task. But from there, month by month, Lucas could sense him gradually loosening the reins, ceding some authority. They still found it difficult to talk, to touch on anything of emotional depth, but at least they were trying. It was progress. Lucas began to take a special interest in the supply chain, their land and holdings abroad, eastern Europe in particular.

As if his stars and planets had shifted into happier alignment, it was soon after this that Suzie entered his life. From across the marquee at his schoolmate Dougie's wedding reception. Flying into his arms at the ceilidh — spinning and laughing in a dance that neither wished to escape from. Nor had they. Four months later they were engaged. Everyone — his parents included — adored her. Now, a year on, they were closing in on those same vows themselves. Just twenty-two days. He was counting off each one.

❧

Thinking of her, Lucas pulled out his phone and hit speed-dial. How cool was this, to talk to her from up here! — The McAllister outpost. Part of their future.

For a moment there was nothing. No sound bar the flap and settle of rooks overhead, the light crunch of their footsteps as Radu led on through the trees, steeply down. Lucas was conscious of the ache in his knees and with a smile imagined Savage berating him, appalled how unfit he'd become. *C'mon*, he muttered into the phone. But just as he assumed the ridges, the dense woods around them, were screwing with the signal, here was her voice, magically clear.

'Luke? — is that you? Jesus! How's it going, baby? Where are you?'

He heard the chatter of children behind her, a corridor echo. Mid-morning break. Could picture her, pile of books beneath an arm, phone in the other, hurrying to the staff-room.

'You won't believe what I'm seeing, Suze. This view. God, I wish you were here . . .'

'Me too, you know that.'

'We'll do it. Soon, I promise.'

'What about the meeting? Have you seen him yet'

'That's at 2:00. We're heading there now.'

'Well, stay cool, honey.'

His father had warned him about Marin, the factory manager; that he needed firm handling.

Don't try to be his friend — you're not. Ask what he needs and he'll take that as weakness. Just tell him what's required . . .

Quality control appeared to be waning. The level of finish: wardrobes, tables, dressers. Lucas came armed with an ultimatum. Any returns from Marin's next shipment, McAllister's would take its business elsewhere. This was leverage, too, for other concessions. Swifter delivery, lower costs. The usual squeeze. Only this time he, Lucas, was ringmaster, running the show. He had no doubt he could do it. It was simply hard to believe still, after all that had gone before. To find himself in this position.

'Better go,' he was saying, 'we're almost at the car . . .'

'Ok . . . but you be careful.'

'C'mon, sweetheart, relax. It's Romania, not Afghanistan.'

Suzie fretted, it was part of her nature. More than once recently he'd dreamt of a bird, hovering just above him, beating its wings in a protective fan. Sometimes he woke convinced it was her, but said nothing. Before the fog of dementia began to absorb his mother, she had been equally protective. Then Suzie had appeared, right on cue, as if stepping into her shoes. In this regard, at least, he'd sought to discourage it. He was his own man now. And though to date he'd kept it to himself, part of him was needled by what her anxiety implied—that at some level he remained vulnerable, naïve, exposed, in particular once they were apart. Lucas loved her to a fault, but still. He knew one thing: he didn't need a new protector, any kind of surrogate parent.

'Miss you, Luke.' Her voice was so close he could sense her, all but smell the scent on her neck.

'You too,' he replied. He could see the 4x4 now. Past Radu's shoulder, fifty metres ahead: a silver gleam at the roadside. 'Love you loads. And don't worry, I'll be fine. See you Wednesday, huh?'

He'd had a beer or two, tried a couple of bars before reaching *No Problem*. The idea was one final drink then back to the hotel. He'd been up since six and fatigue was kicking in fast. He could feel the weight of his bones, a similar heaviness in the eyes. A good day, but already too long. And his next stop tomorrow, a meeting in Oradea on a cheaper source of beech, meant an early ride up to Bacau for the mid-morning flight.

The sound of jazz, a clarinet, lured him inside. The main bar area was packed — most appeared to be students — with the three-piece just visible through the melée, framed by an alcove at the back. A good vibe.

At length he had his glass of Noroc. Edged his way through the crowd and up some steps to a large covered terrace overlooking the street. There were twenty-odd tables, most already full. A slightly older crowd: young professionals, some art-school types. Off in one corner a couple of soaks sat nursing their beers. Ignoring one another they stared down at the street as though they missed it already, the mid-evening strollers with their pockets of coins.

Toward late-afternoon the air had grown noticeably heavier, more oppressive. Each step of his tour at the mill, through the factory, even in discussion with Marin (seated in his glass-walled office overlooking the assembly area, wood-bladed fan turning pointlessly above them) Lucas had sensed his energy draining away.

Now, spotting a free chair and crossing toward it, he detected some cooling at last. A welcome breeze stirred the canopy overhead. The other two couples at the table nodded at his request—sure, go ahead, the seat's vacant. He thanked them, half-turned the chair to afford them a semblance of privacy, and sat down to take in those around him.

A Miles Davis cover drifted up from the bar. From all around him came the contented gabble of voices. Waves of laughter broke across the terrace. The stir of air bore cigarette smoke, perfume, the burn of rubber and gasoline as another local schmuck put his foot to the pedal, screeched away below.

All in all, he was pleased with how it had gone. As his father had warned, Marin was phlegmatic, po-faced, certainly no pushover. Subtlety and charm were wasted on him. Word had it that, twenty-odd years ago, he'd raised a glass briefly to Ceasescu's demise — but nothing since then had provoked as much as a smile. Through their one-hour meeting his expression barely changed: a flat, heavy-lidded stare that gave little away. As far as Lucas was concerned he was either a wily old bastard, a natural for poker who'd missed his real calling, or a fool who'd got lucky, risen way past his pay-grade. Recent history here was littered with those. In the final analysis it mattered little, of course, since Lucas held all the cards . . .

Through the chatter, he was suddenly aware of raised voices. A few metres away a tanned guy was arguing with a girl across the table. He was young, maybe twenty, peroxide hair pulled back in a ponytail. Tall and sinewy, tattooed on each biceps. The sleeveless white T-shirt designed to display his physique. And now he was standing, the table still between them, jabbing a finger at her as he spoke. Lucas's Romanian was basic but the outburst didn't need translation. The volley of insults continued, breaking here and there into the brutally familiar... *beetch!* . . . *slut!* . . . *leetle whore!*

Even as Lucas watched, the girl seemed to shrink before the invective. Pale-skinned, petite, spiky black hair — she'd hunched in her shoulders, drawn up one whip-thin knee then the other, was hugging herself into a ball on her chair.

What a prick, Lucas thought. Something about the guy — preening muscles, brazen aggression, ridiculous tan — really got under his skin. Before he was conscious of doing so, Lucas had risen to his feet, taken four or five steps and found himself beside them. It took just a couple of seconds. The youth paused, looked him up and down. He exuded meanness, tightly wound. But Lucas had committed himself: there was no way back.

'So? What you want?'

A challenge, spat in Romanian. His eyes were chips of hot asphalt. They played over Lucas, sizing him up. A little smirk of dismissal. 'Piss away, yes?' he added in English, turning back to the girl.

Lucas still hadn't spoken. Wondered what it was that tagged him so clearly 'from elsewhere.' Or simply out of his depth.

The idiot started in again, upbraiding her. Lucas was close enough now to feel the guy's body heat, smell the alcohol in his sweat. He'd clearly had a skinful, maybe drugs too, judging by how his eyes darted. When he lunged forward suddenly and grabbed the girl's hair, tried to yank her out of her seat — 'Right now . . .we go!' - Lucas reached out instinctively, knocked his arm away.

'Enough,' he said firmly.

The guy wheeled around. Registered a moment's surprise, then took a swing. Lucas saw it coming, swayed back and avoided it comfortably.

'Whoa . . . take it easy.' He held up his hands. 'I'm out of here. Just give her a break, OK? What kind of guy are you?'

Eyes closed, cupped hands to her ears, the girl began to emit a low, self-contained moan, was rocking lightly back and forth, blocking out what she could. The youth glanced about him. His anger still boiled but he seemed undecided now, an animal caught in the headlights. Lucas, too, became aware that most of the tables were watching them; realised how quiet the terrace had become. The awning flapped overhead. He caught a distant rumble of thunder.

'You . . .' came a softer voice. 'It is you who are leaving.'

The girl had lifted her head, was peering timidly over her still-folded arms, the barrier of her knees. Her eye-liner had run. Lucas could see she was trembling.

'Get away from me, Vasile. Bastard *jerk*!' Her chin wobbled. 'You don't see me again, understand? Not fucking *ever*!'

Lucas wondered if, hearing him, she'd reverted to English for his benefit. He detected a trace of faux-American, as if she'd learnt it from NYPD or the movies. The guy was still simmering, but cornered; aware the game was up. He looked from the girl to Lucas and back again.

'*Ai sa regreti târfa!*' jabbing that finger at her again, '*poti fii sigura!*'

He backed into a chair behind him. Threw its occu-pant—a severe-looking woman in a damson blouse—a look of sheer hatred. Then spun away, hurried off between the tables. Lucas watched him disappear down the steps before turning back to the girl. Conversation—doubtless on one topic only—resumed swiftly around them.

'You OK?' he asked, squatting down beside her, resting a hand on her shoulder. Slowly she unwrapped her arms from her knees, lowered bare feet to the floor. He was struck by how small they were, by the tiny high-heels beneath the table, one lying on its side.

'He is gone?' A small but resilient voice; a little scratchy and hoarse.

Lucas nodded. 'You alright?' he repeated.

'Sure . . . I . . .'

She was still trembling. And now he could sense her

embarrassment kicking in too. The way she avoided his gaze, sniffled and wiped at her eyes. Leaned over and fished in her bag for a tissue, cigarettes.

'Thank you,' she said, looking up at him finally. Her eyes were red-rimmed, smudgy with mascara, but a striking aqueous green. 'Is a kind thing you do.' With a smoker's urgency she tapped a cigarette from the pack, cupped her hands round the lighter, drew the hit in deep.

'I didn't mean to butt in, it's just . . .'

'No, please,' she blew smoke. 'You can see . . . this guy is a moron.'

Lucas smiled. There was steeliness there, she hadn't had the fight beaten out of her, and this pleased him. All the same he felt suddenly awkward: over-conscious of his hands, what to do with them. Locating the back pockets of his jeans, he shoved them in, gave a little shrug.

'Pretty much. That's maybe too kind to him.'

She seemed to find this amusing—a half-cough, half-chuckle catching in her throat.

'Hah. Vasile is not liking kindness,' she answered. 'Come, please . . .' she waved a hand at the now-vacant chair, a coil of bangles jingling on her wrist. A miracle they stay there, he thought, she's that damn skinny. 'I am Katya. Sit with me. Just for a minute . . .'

He hesitated, shifting his hands to the back of the chair. 'Thanks, Katya. I'm Lucas. Or Luke . . . people call me both. I don't know about you, but I need a drink.' He nodded at her empty glass. 'What was in there?'

'No-no, I will buy.' Again she waved her hand languidly. Picked up a shoulder-bag, set it down on her lap and delved in again. 'But not here. I have to get out of this place.'

As she bent forward he noticed a single slim braid at the back of her neck: a few inches long, like a dark mouse's tail. With the movement of her head it fell forward onto one shoulder, hung there for a second till she flicked it unconsciously back. Fishing out a compact she brought the mirror up to her face, checking each profile. Dabbed on some powder, a touch of fresh lipstick; clipped it shut.

'Come,' she said, rising. 'I know a nice place, very close.'

'Listen, maybe I should . . .'

Duty done, tomorrow flitted back into mind, the early start, but hearing his hesitation she threw him a look — half-pout, half-smile — that disarmed him. Given what she had been through, her still-fragile state, it did seem mildly ungracious to abandon her at once. There was no doubt, too, that this sudden turn of events — the adrenalin still pulsing through him — had shaken him out of himself, given him a fresh shot of energy. Out of nowhere the night had opened up a new path, the kind he'd always been alert to, relished exploring. And, yes, part of him was curious, keen to know more about this strange little creature he'd . . . well, if not rescued, at least risked a blow or two for. Had she been here, witnessed what had happened, he knew that Suzie would feel much the same. Above all, though, she'd be proud of what he had done; of the courage that, truth be told, surprised even him.

So he found himself down on the street, a good head and shoulders above her as they walked, the click of her heels amplified by the precinct. Drops of rain began to spot the pavement. Looking up, he welcomed their coolness on his face. It was hard to make out the sky through the streetlights but whatever was up there seemed unnaturally dark. The air was charged. One could smell the storm coming.

'Who was that guy anyway?' he asked. 'A boyfriend?'

This time her glance was of deep irritation, almost disgust. '*Tch*. Vasile? No way! He follow me for years, even in High School. Sure, he *like* to be boyfriend. But he is . . . he is a creep, yes? Think he own me. We fight many time like this, but tonight . . .' She hissed with frustration, waved a thin arm dramatically—a gesture he already sensed was habitual. Her bangles tinkled again like a rain-stick. 'Tonight I tell him 'no more.' Is finish. Or I find the police.'

She pointed, nudged him to the right. They crossed the street and turned the next corner. Somewhere off in the hills a thunderflash lit the sky, followed a few seconds later by the echoing rumble, rolling in like distant artillery fire.

Glancing across he caught her watching him; narrowing her eyes as if weighing him up.

'What is it?' he laughed.

'You have business here? In Onesti?'

Shed of collar and tie, his corporate demeanour, he wondered how she could tell. Was he really that obvious?

'No tourist come here,' she went on. 'Is nothing to see, only factory. And many they close. Little jobs little money. Most boring town in Romania I think . . .'

Lucas smiled. 'C'mon, surely not?' He trawled his head fast, what he'd read before the trip; came up with the town's one claim to fame. 'Nadia Comaneci . . . she was born here, right?'

'Is true,' Katya shrugged. 'And where is she now? America, of course.'

That was good. She was clear-eyed, sardonic, no bullshit. And there were many worse guides to a town. Lucas decided he liked her.

'Well, you're right. I'm here for the timber. Trees, furniture . . . you know?' He mimed clumsily at wielding an axe and at once felt an idiot. But she seemed to get it.

'Dinescu's? Big place, near the river?'

He nodded.

'Many used to work there. My uncle, two cousin . . .' She clicked her tongue. 'They send them all home, three years ago maybe. Now is only machine.'

'I'm sorry . . . I don't really know,' he said, keen to steer her from the subject. Radical restructuring, new plant—they'd been a condition of his father's investment when he acquired the majority shareholding. 'I'm here just a couple of days. Leaving tomorrow, in fact. Oradea, then on to Budapest. More meetings.' He lifted his shoulders. 'Duller than Onesti, I assure you.'

She didn't smile or respond. Her attention seemed to drift in and out. It probably wasn't true about Hungary, in any case. That was the meeting he awaited most eagerly; where he'd need to impress them, be sharp, but from where he could also set the seal on his father's approval, bring home the main prize. A new direction and partnership for the business: cabin-like homes in kit-form, self-assembled, almost half the price of the Scandinavian equivalent. He and his father agreed that the product, its quality, was excellent. Now Lucas was charged with assessing the Hungarian directors, their operation, in person. Were they trustworthy, men one could work with? If so, to sound out the numbers, something to inform their first bid.

'But what about you?' he asked Katya.

She'd stopped across the street from a glowing doorway. Outside it a couple of doormen—regular musclemen in tuxedos, polished pates glistening like snooker balls—were processing a line of would-be clubbers.

She turned and smiled, looked up at him directly. Another faintly challenging look, head cocked to one side. The little black dress merely emphasised her fragility, her diminutive stature. In the half-light she seemed almost androgynous, he reflected, more like an adolescent boy.

'What about me, Luke?'

It was strange, hearing his name on her tongue. He felt disconcerted again, but it was, after all, a fair question. He did wonder who she was, what she did; and why it was he was following her through this godforsaken town in an unfamiliar country. He stood there shaking his head as she looked at him quizzically. How strange life was, he thought. From one second to the next you never knew where it would lead. But thank God for that.

'Well . . . I just meant . . . I get the feeling drama follows you around. You're something creative, I'm sure. An actor . . .a dancer maybe? Am I right?'

Still smiling, she slipped an arm through his.

'You are good, Luke. Very good. I am artist, designer . . . in the college. Always I am painting, since little girl.' She gave him a gentle tug forward. 'Now, come to meet other good people. These are my friends.'

She led him straight to the front of the line. One of the bouncers, his over-tight jacket set to burst from it's one straining button, beamed at her approach, eased a couple aside to let them through. Katya paused, gave the grizzled bear a peck on one cheek—she on tiptoe, he bending forward as she murmured in his ear. When the man shot him an amused glance, growled something back at her as they passed on, Lucas knew it was about him. But the only word he recognised was her name.

He followed her down the steep flight of steps beneath flashing neon that announced this as *Underground*. Grace Jones was extolling 'La Vie En Rose' to greet them. Lucas smiled to himself. Life had rarely felt better, for sure.

At the foot of the stairs, through an arch to one side, he glimpsed an intimate candlelit room, twenty-odd people at dinner. He followed Katya away from them to where the space opened out on a small curving counter, a dozen or so customers sipping drinks, talking, some perched on bar-stools. Downlight shimmered off the back mirror and hammered chrome counter, the shelves of bottles and glasses. Three or four barmen, their shirts a luminous white, moved around one another like practised sailors in their galley, mixing, pouring, replenishing. The crypt-like space stretched away from them in a series of flickering alcoves. Each framed or partly concealed couples and groups — maybe fifty people in all — already well-chilled in deep leather sofas, armchairs. Ambient music hovered behind the laughter and conversation, though from somewhere, as if deeper underground, came the muffled thud of a bass-line like the ocean hitting rocks.

'Corona? Noroc? What will you take?' she asked.

'Come on. I can't let you do this . . .'

She shrugged amiably, pressed the 50-*lei* note discreetly into his fingers. 'Is OK, I wait over here. For me is the vodka with apple . . .' and moved off to look for a seat.

Just as she claimed, she wasn't short of friends here. In the next hour or so he lost count of how many — men and women equally — caught sight of her, called out her name. Made their way to the nook that she'd found, or her spot on the dance-floor, threw their arms open to kiss and embrace her. Rangy, silken-haired girls who, if they weren't models, aspired to be. The full spectrum from out-and-out camp to stud-collars, piercings and chains. The one thing they shared was style. Possibly only here, safe from judgement, could they raise the panache to carry it off; but whatever they exuded — true pride perhaps, confidence in their own skin — there was something about them Lucas envied.

At first he rose and smiled at each, nodded in greeting, shook hands. But after a while it was pointless. One blurred to the next. He knocked back the contents of the shot glass before him. It tasted of berries, wild berries with a kick. The deepest of reds, almost black, the colour of blood. Marec, Ioan, Elie, Silviu: names drifted by him with a line or two of their stories, how their paths and Katya's had crossed, but in truth he was happier once each had moved on.

He relaxed, felt some kind of equilibrium restored. And he'd earned it, hadn't he — a couple more drinks? He was well in control, would shortly wish her goodnight, content she was safe and secure now, his duty accomplished.

They chinked glasses again.

'I am thinking now, Luke . . . you remind me of someone.'

'I do?'

'*Da*, for sure. This guy I see in the movie sometime. He is from Denmark, I think. Targo Hansen.'

Lucas had never seen or heard of the guy. Nonetheless, the name jolted him a little. He'd no use for, rarely thought of, what had to be there on his birth certificate, wherever that was. *Lucas H McAllister*. Back when he was ten or eleven the scabby crew he'd hung out with (he could still picture one or two) took to calling him 'H' for a while till the novelty passed. Ribbing him with absurd and scurrilous guesses, maddened by his refusal to say what it stood for. His old man's Dad had been Lucas, and Hansen his mother's maiden name. And now, with this cute and curious woman studying him closely, he almost blurted it out, confessed to this mildly diverting coincidence. But just as it had with his mates and tormentors those light-years ago, some instinct prevented him. True though it was, sometimes the truth just sounds too unlikely, and he feared her thinking he was one for cheap lines. As when Katya had touched on his work, he was set on keeping his distance, nothing too personal. His real life lay elsewhere. She had a good impression of him; he was happy to leave it at that.

'Your paintings, Katya. What are they like?' For some reason he imagined huge and wild abstracts in oil—blazing primary colours.

'I paint only the body,' she smiled. 'This is what I love.'

'Ah, life studies, you mean? Portraits?'

'No, no,' she shook her head, still amused. 'The body, Luke. The real body.' She tapped at her breastbone.

He was grasping it slowly but still slightly non-plussed.

'I start a few years ago... just with the nails . . .' She held out a hand, showed him her own. On each was a different design in red, blue and yellow. Stars, little flags. The national colours.

'Cool,' he said, taking her hand to examine it.

'. . . later friends say I must try on the body. Now I do all—make painting, tattoo. The body is my . . .' she took back her hand, waved it in little circles, groping for the word, 'uggh... how you say this?'

'Your canvas,' Lucas nodded.

'*Da*, that is it. Soon my dream is to have my own place — you know, for the work? And one day,' she smiled, withdrawing her hand, 'many shop with my name. Not just Romania . . . Budapest, Paris, Berlin... everywhere, Luke!'

'Sure, why not. Here's to you, Katya,' he raised his glass. 'Hope it works out. London too?'

'But of course. Always I wish to see London, since I was small . . .'

Before each glass was quite empty it appeared to be filled again. She was bright, fun to talk to, certainly no strain on the eye. Her smoker's voice seemed to coat all she said in thick honey, made him want to hear more. And it came to him slowly that she too brought to mind a face he'd all but forgotten.

There'd been a girl called Ellie, a class or two above him, the first girl who turned his heart over. He must have been around twelve. In one sense they were insepa-rable — he trailed her like a puppy wherever she went, in school and out (my God, he winced at the shame of it; worse still, his childish parallel with Katya's crazed stalker) — but in almost a year, before Ellie won a schol-arship to some impossibly glamorous place and vanished from his life overnight, he'd said barely ten words to her. He doubted any had registered. She never spoke to him.

He half-expected Katya to grasp what he was thinking, to leap up and bolt for it, run a mile from him also. And yet, as she revealed some of her own frustrations (raised in a largely illiterate village, her desperation to escape — like him a lone child on whom every hope and disappoint-ment had fallen) he wanted to tell her they had more in common than she knew. Over the next hour or so as they drank and danced in the adjacent, strobe-lit den — her body-heat, the crowd's, the relentless trance-beat and the tabs of acid she laid like hosts on their tongues — it all spun him to a place where her green eyes breathed and the room itself smiled and caressed them with colour — he could have told her anything and everything, and prob-ably had. He felt the energy glow and surge right through him, build as he moved, sweep up his spine and burst from his head like a flower.

Then, suddenly parched, he was in the Men's Room, splashing water over his face, gulping down handfuls. Lifting his head he confronted someone vaguely familiar in the glass, watched the beads and rivulets crawl down its face like tiny blind insects. He reached up to them cautiously, eyes still fixed in the mirror. Dabbed shakily at them, convinced his skin itself was dissolving, falling away like some mutant chameleon's. But he — or this other — continued to grin lopsidedly, to revel in it all. The strange rictus spreading, distorting its features.

You have to get back. The phrase was burrowing through his head. And there was a girl. He should be back with the girl. Fumbling away from the basins he screwed up his eyes in an effort to remember. What was her name? The word *tomorrow* was flashing before him too, something vaguely important, and then Suzie's face (Suzie, that was it) and his chest was full of needles, lots of tiny needles, and he knew his task was to climb, climb up and out, find the soft place prepared for him, wherever that was . . .

One moment the long light above him was flickering and jumping, all part of the message, then it was gone and the tight fragrant space was just darkness. Other masses and shapes stumbled blindly around and against him, cursing in various tongues. Lucas gripped the stanchion of a stall and waited, uncertain he could stand any longer unaided. A power-cut, yes . . . you just had to wait. And sure enough, within a few seconds, back came the light with a wavering, uncertain glow.

He made it back to the bar, slumping down beside Katya just as the process repeated itself to a huge boom of thunder outside. It seemed nothing worth heeding, not when light and sound had shimmered and sparkled all evening, risen and fallen in tune with the music, the pump of his blood. As the visible came and went, all he heard were whoops and whistles, laughter through the gloom. The tea-lights on the tables trembled and winked in their bowls like a hundred red eyes, casting shadows and silhouettes, picking out ghoulish faces.

The strap of his watch, catching on his jeans as he reached for his glass, was another small jolt: a moment's recognition of something beyond them, a door barely opening.

'I must . . . I should really . . .' he murmured.

Before he'd uttered the words they were drowned by a series of shouts, barked orders, the clump of boots on the stairs. Then he was blinded, harsh tunnels of torchlight sweeping the room. Instinctively he pulled Katya upright, trying to shield his eyes. His head swam.

'*Duceti-va! Repede! Acum!*'

Two men in caps, uniforms, had leapt onto the bar, their torch-beams searching the cavernous space. Women began to shriek and whimper. Lucas was aware that the music next door had ceased altogether. All around them people were scattering.

Shit, he thought, it's a bust. Cops after dealers, intent on pinning them to the floor, kicking butt.

'Hold on,' he told Katya, trying to shake himself alert. His voice seemed to come from a distance. He took hold of her wrist. 'Don't let go, OK?'

Propelled by the nightmare of his name on a rap-sheet, calling home from the cells, he dragged her out of their seat, jolting into others, invisible furniture, toward his recollection of the exit. He could make it out in one of the beams along with a sound like a freight train approaching. And now his feet, his ankles were suddenly cold, heavy as anchors, they seemed to be wading through water. But it still took a moment — his first glimpse of the stairs, figures scrambling, fighting upward as the flood hammered in with the force of a cataract—to realise they actually were.

Barged back and forth in the crush, stumbling and splashing, by the time they reached the foot of the stairs and could grab at the handrail the bottom two steps were already submerged. And then it was like climbing a water-fall—Katya before him, clinging to the rail, buffeted to her knees as he shoved her up and forward, as he too was propelled from behind by the desperate clamour of bodies. It took maybe a minute—sliding back, crawling on. Once they emerged, clothes plastered in a tight freez-ing sheath to their skin, there was no sign of pavement or street, simply more water, a brown surge sucking at their calves, churning and boiling away past the church on the corner. The far side of the street, the hazy outlines of people struggling for cover, were just a blur through the downpour. The whole scene flickered before him like a scratched and disintegrating black-and-white film.

'. . . bridges down . . . back this way . . . ' Lucas caught a few shouted words blowing past, rags in the gale. Vicious, horizontal rain flew at them through the streetlights: he felt as though his face was being pierced by a thousand icy needles. Behind them more and more were spilling from the exit, stumbling from one chaos to another, shoving others aside. He saw a woman knocked to her knees, scrambling and shrieking in the deluge, a red gash across her forehead.

'C'mon, round here . . .'

He pulled Katya with him, away from the bottleneck. A few metres to their right was a junction. With an arm firmly round her they waded toward it, turned the corner and flattened themselves to a wall. Only now, shielded from the squall, could Lucas clear the water from his eyes to check on her properly. She seemed even smaller beside him now, cut off at the knees by the flood. Shivering, bedraggled, hair flattened to her skull. Down a face washed of colour, eyeliner ran like black tears. The outline of her ribs, her small breasts, showed clearly through the saturated dress.

'How you doing?' He tried to smile reassurance but his face was numb, wouldn't work. 'OK so far?'

She hugged herself, teeth chattering, but surprised him even now. Smiling back, wiping almost dreamily at her face with the back of her hand

'How . . . how much could this happen, Luke? We only now meet and you . . . you rescue me again. Is really something, yes?'

'Shit, Katya. This is no joke. Look at us. Look at this.' He waved an arm at the rows of parked cars, water now up to their sills. Some were already rocking like boats in a swell, keen to slip their moorings. He had to reach out, take hold of a lamp-post to keep his footing. Out where the road had been a couple of dustbins, a twisted tree-limb swept rapidly past—followed, as though giving chase, by the bobbing dark head of a dog. Muzzle held high, struggling for air, it was still yapping weakly. They stood there helpless, watching it go.

'Here, c'mon.' He held his hand out to Katya and she took it. 'I told you not to let go.'

'My handbag, my shoes... ' She looked around as if they might magically reappear.

'Where do you live?' he asked, pulling her close, struggling to focus.

She nodded vaguely. 'Over there . . . Calea Belvedere. By cathedral.'

'Is it near?'

She shook her head, tried to point, but her arm was

like a rag doll's. 'Across town. I find taxi maybe . . .' Her voice trailed away.

'Oh, right.' He swore under his breath. She was still stoned, for chrissake; either that or in shock. Maybe they both were. Hell, if they waited here a while, let the receptors and dopamine settle, it could all just prove a bad trip. They'd come to in those deep leather cushions, grab another drink and head back to the dance floor . . .

But the cold was his answer. He was too damn cold—chilled to the bone, getting colder.

'Forget taxis.' He almost had to shout for her to hear him over the rush of water, the moan of the wind. 'We need a fucking boat. And I don't see any of those.' C'mon…time to go.'

Without thinking—he could see there was no other option—he bent and lifted her into his arms. Fortunately, she weighed next to nothing. The current was formidable now and he needed all his strength to stay balanced.

'*Doamne Dumnezeule!*' She gave a shriek. 'My God, Luke, where do you take me . . .?' But despite it all—his uncertain steps through the maelstrom below her, rain that lashed on without mercy—she began to giggle again.

'My hotel,' he told her, 'it's just a couple of blocks, I think we can make it . . .'

He hoped to God he was right. So far the water was only just up to his calves but with each step he took he could feel the surge strengthen, trying to suck off his shoes. It was all he could do to hold her, never mind move forward.

'Sorry, girl. It's not going to work.' He set her down, gently as he could, in the icy flood; she gave a little yelp as her bare feet re-entered the water. 'C'mon,' he pulled her in tight to his side, took her with him.

She splashed and stumbled along in the crook of his

arm, muttering to herself. When she'd led him to the club his impression had been of a fairly small circle from where he'd set out, earlier in the evening. If so, the Hotel Deva was just a block or two to the left, but he couldn't get much sense from her now. Her words were muffled by his shirt — by the rain as it whipped and hammered whatever it could — and what language she was using, God only knew. All that sustained him was the vision of his room, how it would feel to be warm again, dry.

They edged forward, step by step, as the water swirled about them. He kept close to the railings and walls where he knew it was paved underfoot. Each time one of them staggered or lunged they could reach out and steady themselves, press on again. His first target was the corner past the church and sure enough, having turned it, they were finally out of the worst of the current, able to move with more confidence. Now at last he began to recognise things: the woman's boutique just ahead, its mannequins bobbing gently against the display-glass; the BCR Bank across the street. Groping past it to the hotel steps (still a few feet above water) he wondered how many *lei* would soon be floating free from tills and vaults across town.

He set her down carefully under the portico as rain continued to lash in between the columns. Her bare feet struggled for grip and he steadied her again. Then the glass doors slid open before them and they stood there a moment, exposed to the plush and pristine lobby like actors caught out by an unscheduled curtain-rise. Making laughable efforts to straighten drenched clothing, run hands through dripping, wind-tangled hair, they stepped inside. A pair of bellhops hurried toward them across the marble, expressions caught between amazement and alarm. Lucas steered Katya, hunched and shivering, to the desk, a pooling trail in their wake.

'. . . but Mr Lucas . . . my God.' The night manager stood his ground behind the desk like a captain on the bridge of his ship. 'And the *doamna* . . . she is OK?'

'She'll be fine . . . just fine. A hot bath, that's all . . .' Only now did Lucas realise how much he was trembling too. He nodded at the pigeon-holes. '308, please.'

'Is not safe to be out there.' The manager handed him the swipe card, nodding at a screen that flickered on a shelf behind the desk. Through the newscast's jumping, distorted picture, its own storm of interference, Lucas made out the nightmare they'd escaped from. Churning water, buckled trees. Firemen, police. It was hardly news to him.

'*Multumesc*,' he answered. 'Don't worry, we're staying put. But that taxi's still booked for tomorrow, yes?'

The man peered over his half-moon glasses, consulting lists beneath the counter.

'It is here,' he tapped at the paper. '8:30am. Though of course . . .' He shrugged, glancing outside. 'Let us hope the storm passes.'

'For sure,' Lucas echoed. He placed a hand lightly in the small of Katya's back and steered her to the lift. One of the bellhops had the doors open and waiting.

Then finally they were there in the room, this door closing behind them with a soft, secure click. The warmth and quiet were vivid, intense. Water still ran from them freely, darkening the light blue carpet. Lucas threw off his jacket—it came off his back like a bag of wet cement—made straight for the bathroom and turned on the shower. Lifting two towels from the rail, he came back and passed one to Katya.

'Go on,' he told her, 'get in and warm up.' She was still shaking but her face wore a half-dazed grin of relief. 'When you're done, you take the bed. I'll be fine here with a blanket.' He gestured at the armchair then reached out and touched her cheek reassuringly. 'You're quite safe, I promise.'

She shook out the towel, rubbed it absently over her dishevelled hair. Took a step closer. He looked down at her feet, her toes like tiny blind fish in the blue. The smile was still there as she raised a hand slowly, traced his lips with her finger.

'You are really sweet man, Luke. You know this? But maybe,' and now she raised her eyes too, their startling and watery green, looking right into his like a challenge, 'maybe safe is not how I want . . .'

There was a pause in which new sheets of rain hit the glass, peppered it like grapeshot. Steam drifted in from the bathroom. Her pelvis, hard and bony, brushed his thigh and steam seemed to rise from her also — her skin, her dress — as she warmed.

This was the moment. For an hour or two at least it had lain in some crevice at the back of his thoughts, the eel beneath the rock. He'd known it was there but had felt no anxiety, confident that if the time came he could handle it, swim easily away. And here was the time. Over her shoulder he glimpsed his bags open on the stand beneath the window. Barely unpacked, ready for the fast zip shut, another early departure.

'No, Katya, no . . .'

He took her wrist gently, tried to lower her hand. Find the words to explain why it just wasn't possible. But his head was still scrambled, his limbs numb — in every sense now she had him off-balance. Before he knew what had happened she'd pushed him back on the bed with sudden and extraordinary force, was astride him, pinning his wrists, her legs like steel coils, her tongue now the eel against his.

'Oh God . . .'

He couldn't tell if he said it out loud but in an instant—too high, tired or weak to resist—all the fight went out of him. He felt himself dissolving beneath her, her eager and tough little frame. Knew that all he'd reclaimed was already blown away, straws in the gale. There was nothing left to cling to. He let go and fell.

Then it was brutal, unstoppable. They tore and clawed at each other, tumbling from mattress to floor, thudding into the wall. As she clambered and rode and smeared herself over him he tasted blood on his lips, felt them swollen and bruised. But her boldness inflamed him, the salty musk of her pores. Their shared sweat and heat was oil on the fire. In her desperate kiss he could taste the whole night—its fear and relief. Bittersweet, smoky, mingled with rain.

Not even her strangest secret deflected him. Every part of her hidden till now bore its mark—a mazing of scars, dark ridges and welts, half-healed cuts that roughened her torso and back, her breasts and behind. His first thought was Vasile, the pig: some form of vicious, demented abuse for which he should swing. Lucas grasped her still tighter in pity and rage. Astonished, compelled, his hands and tongue traced her like braille, each livid scab standing proud of the skin. But the deeper and longer he explored, the more intimate they became, the wounds seemed to speak to him otherwise; to shift before his eyes into ever-changing patterns, diagrams, maps that he couldn't decipher. Razor-fine, scored with precision and purpose. Now they were letters and numbers, kenji or Mandarin. Criss-crossing her belly, the ladder of her back. Tribal markings, badges of courage . . .

Maybe it was simply exhaustion, the acid's lysergic residue working the last of its magic, but as they flung themselves apart, gasping like divers breaking the surface, his last conscious thought was that the message of her body was her life and his, the story of them both.

At some point he awoke.

For some moments he lay there, flat on his back, listening to the wind, the unceasing rain that beat at the window. He had no idea where he was. It was only as he tried to sit up, found that he couldn't, that he opened his eyes. They felt hard and dead as two stones, behind which a colony of ants were busily at work.

Through the half-drawn curtains a sudden thunderflash lit up the room. He raised his head again cautiously, a few inches from the pillow; looked down the length of his body. Then to each side, along his outstretched arms. What he saw made him pray he was dreaming. Spread-eagled, naked, his wrists were held fast, fastened to the narrow steel bedposts. Same with his ankles. It looked like some kind of cable-tie, a beaded black plastic or nylon. Instinctively he jerked back and forth, wincing with pain as the beads seemed to tighten, bite deeper into his flesh. Sharp as razor-wire.

Desperate, whimpering, he caught a glimpse of his briefcase, the overnight bag, just as the room returned to shadow. Both were tipped open, all but empty, papers and clothing strewn across the floor.

And then he remembered.

'Katya!' he shouted. His throat was parched, his voice hoarse. She was long gone, he knew. Probably with anything of value—his passport and wallet, his mobile—he knew that too. Maybe even the tickets.

Comaneci's town, he thought. Where one's only dream is to leave.

The room was getting colder. More likely it was him — immobile, exposed, their heat an evaporated memory. He looked across for the phone on the nightstand — not that he knew how to reach it — but even that wasn't there. He called out for help, several times, yelling as loud as he could. When nobody came he wondered if there were other guests there, below or above him, in the neighbouring rooms. If they could have heard him in any case, through the storm or their sleep. He wanted someone to come yet dreaded them finding him. No explanation was equal to this. And how would they take it? Which sent his thoughts straight to Suzie, his father. Prayer was all he had left and he tried it; but even this felt as futile.

Summoning what strength he could, he made one final effort. Threw his weight hard, left and right, trying to shake the whole bed. But the frame was too heavy, held in place by the carpet, and his movement too limited to have any effect. All he managed to do was wrench both his shoulders, bite his lip from the pain that shrieked through him, taste blood.

Resigned, he fell back again, crushed with self-pity. He'd simply gone to her aid, after all. Was this fair, given all he had to lose? If he hadn't walked into that place, if the storm had held off for an hour or so longer, none of this would've happened. His eyes prickled with tears. All it had required was resolve, a modicum of disciple. Faith in who he'd become, what he and Suzie had. But this was all beyond him now. As was she.

From the moment he'd approached Katya's table, had she planned the whole thing? He even pictured her and Vasile, somewhere out there together, laughing their heads off. What hurt most was the spectre of his father, to think he'd been right all along. He didn't have what it took to steward himself, never mind the company, a wife.

He felt terrified, appalled. And yet, in a way he found inexplicable, strangely relieved.

Blood thudding in his temple and chest he lay and listened to the rain, hard as hail against the glass. It was all he could do. Wait for daybreak to come, the first sounds from the corridors, other rooms. The eventual knock of the housemaid, click of her pass-key.

All that would follow.

Monkey Knife Fight

THEY REACHED THE knoll around twilight, hunkered down in the brush. Below them the little cage rattled along, making its last sweep down the driving range. Beyond, through the trees, pinpoints of light flickered brightly from the clubhouse.

'I told you, lose the hat!' Ski hissed. 'You look like a goddam traffic-light.'

Strike narrowed his eyes, glanced darkly across. What was needed was a swift and cutting response but nothing came to him and the moment passed.

'. . . *like Cortez on his fucking peak . . .*' Ski muttered, '*a bonfire on a hill . . .*'

Strike sighed, clicked his tongue. Back in High School, Detroit, Ski may have skipped class, spent more time dodging the cops—well, that was his story—but where words were concerned he still had it, there was no competition. Even now, a half-crippled stuntman who to Strike's certain knowledge hadn't worked on-set for a year, he carried these lines and scripts in his head, tossed them out like confetti. Literature, he called it.

'Right. Sure thing,' Strike whispered back. He pulled off his visor and stuffed it into a pocket. 'Remind me, Clooney. How long's it been now? Since Larry called.'

Larry Stein was Ski's agent. Emphasis deep on the *was*.

'Like I said. Waiting's part of the game, kid.' Ski's gaze remained fixed on the cage. The last orange embers were

flickering out on the skyline behind him. Cars slid by
on the beltway. In the sliver of moonlight, perspiration
glistened on his forehead like mercury. 'Same as this. All
about patience . . .'

They'd popped a couple of bennies before heading out,
huffed down a joint. He could still taste the weed on his
breath, smell its smoke in Ski's sweat. Heat pulsed off the
rock-like shadow beside him. The air was still smoth-
ering, a clinging humidity, but it wasn't just that. The
edge remained in Ski's voice. In the last few weeks he'd
claimed often enough to be over it, but that was just gas.
He was still sore as hell and Strike knew it. Nursing his
gripe like a scab, unable to leave it alone. Christ, it was
nearly two months now. He was starting to wonder if
they'd ever get past it.

But for now here they were, trying to hold it together.
Clubs to hand, ready to roll. Bound again by the tres-
passer's rush of adrenalin, two punks on the fly. As if to
confirm it, Ski threw him a quick sideways smirk, whispered: 'Sorry there champ. Kinda wired, huh?'

But that's how he got at these moments. Strike had
seen it all before. No matter what they chose for a fairway:
abandoned yards, empty backstreets or this, the real deal.
They never spoke about why, but both of them knew.
These were his playgrounds, where words meant squat.
The closer they came to teeing it up, Ski would coil
tighter while his own muscles loosened, relaxed, eager
for the task. It was all about confidence and right now he
could sense its return, flooding back with the Demerol.
The turf felt springier under his sneakers, pine-scent burst
behind his eyes, the stars danced to their separate music.
And all the while he could sense Ski's discomfort, seeping
out of his pores like the Humboldt Cryp. With clubs in

their hands he had no answer. Most times he was in for a hiding.

Tonight they'd each brought a five-iron. Travelling light was the key; if you needed an exit-route fast, one club was easy to ditch. And in theory it evened the contest. As ever, though, Ski's equipment was practically new — fucking Mizuno 63's. Like he told it, some golf-nut B-movie actor had called him from the bar at the Clevelander, after some blow. (People in the business, out-of-towners especially, still got in touch when they needed a special delivery, someone to vouch for its quality). A few cocktails later he's leaving with the guy's goddam number, a set of pro tools and a round at Doral. That was Ski. Luck seemed to follow him around. Half-shot as he was — with that creaky, muscle-locked swing — the poor guy had to find an edge somehow. But seeing how his new weapon sparkled like some *Star Wars* ray-gun, he had a nerve too — bleating at another joe's hat.

Strike looked down at his own club, a discarded Titliest, one of several that Ski had pulled from the bag at the back of his room, all those weeks ago. True, he'd since had them re-gripped, been offered more up-to-date models, but so far Strike had resisted. He was used to these now, and there was no greater buzz than taking on the old guy, then taking him down, with pure skill and talent. Watching him fret and twitch, zig-zag and curse round whatever mad route they'd decided. As far as he was concerned, Ski could take the lead, play the big shot all he liked. But when it mattered — on hardpan, tarmac or grass — when it came to these little escapades, they both knew that he had it and Ski did not.

'Shit, c'mon man,' he whispered, shifting impatiently, peering into the murk.

The quiet out here, the wide-open spaces, spooked him a little. All this manicured turf, stands of pine, gnarly oaks with their Spanish moss beards—now he could actually see it all . . . it was like overload, something out of Ski's movies.

'Take it easy. He'll be gone.' Ski spat out the stem of grass he'd been chewing.

At length the beat-up contraption drew up near the hut, spluttering once or twice as it died. A distance off, some creature broke the stillness with a single harsh cry. Together they watched the man's shadow climb out of the cage, secure chain and lock round a massive oak trunk, vanish into the hut. A moment later he was out again, pushing his bike, climbing on, weaving unsteadily off against the pink horizon, a cartoon silhouette.

'OK,' Ski said.

He took the left tree-line, Strike headed right. For two or three minutes they darted back and forth, combing the shadowy ground. Beneath the trees it was knotted and lumpy with roots, covered with pine-cones. Here the machine couldn't operate and range balls lay everywhere, glowing like mushrooms. Just asking to be picked, Strike smiled to himself. His pockets soon bulged with enough for another few rounds.

Ski materialised out of the gloom.

'Guess we're all loaded,' he grinned. 'Lead on, Macduff.'

They moved soundlessly down the bank, round the back of the putting green. From here the cart-path snaked palely away toward the first tee. Another thicket of trees shielded them from the pro-shop and clubhouse. They skirted the edge of a pond that guarded the seventh's huge rolling green. The flagstick was still there, up on the top plateau, motionless as they trotted by. From all around came the croaking of bullfrogs, the electric hum of crickets. Conditions were perfect: warm and still, a curl of new moon overhead. Dark enough to conceal their progress, just enough light to pick out key detail: trees shaping each fairway, the bunkers' shadowy hollows and mounds. Their pace quickened to a jog, each footfall cushioned by the soft spongy grass. Then they were flying; racing each other back to the tee; panting and laughing. Almost like old times. Ski could still shift for a guy in his condition, Strike had to admit. The whole thing was a rush, on a par with any A-grade candy. Out here, club in hand, free and unhindered — the thought flashed in and out of his head that this was true happiness, or close as it came.

They played a couple of regular holes, no problem — down the middle, found their shots fast, no sign of anyone. On the greens they used the iron's leading-edge — two putts max, 'nearest-hole wins.' Scampered to the next tee like souped-up quarterbacks.

'Whoa! Go, honey, go!' Ski really cranked one away down the fifth, a long par five, dogleg left. 'See that, kid? Knock it past *that* little baby!'

Till the last few weeks, this shit about Julie, Strike knew he'd have laughed; read nothing more in the challenge than friendship, innocent goading. Nice soft draw, high easy fade — didn't matter; he could ease it past Ski with his eyes closed. But tonight, he sensed it already, Ski was pushing his buttons, trying to needle him. There was a strange kind of glee in his voice, the way he dummy-boxed him just a little too firm, in the shoulder, as Strike moved by him onto the tee, pushed his peg in the ground.

Faintly, maybe two hundred ahead, he could make out the rushes that marked the turn in the dogleg. Moonlight glittered there too, the edge of a lake.

'Better stand clear, gramps. I'm playin' on through . . .'

He took a quick glance up while addressing the ball — saw Ski's grin vanish, his mouth and jaw begin working, as though he was chewing tough meat. 'Sure, champ,' he muttered, 'you go right ahead . . .'

Strike gripped the club firmly. Set the ball back in his stance, pushed his hands forward. Delofted the face all he could. This would drive the ball forward, hard and low, more like a one-iron. Without thought he opened his stance just a little, closed his shoulders — each small adjustment ensuring a low, raking hook. Then the club moved smoothly away from the ball, no sense of hurry, and returned with an audible crack — the rock-solid contact that by now was his trademark. He felt the ball fizz away off the grooves, the moment of compression and release singing beautifully up through the shaft, up into his hands.

From the first time he picked up a club, gave it a swish, it had just felt right. Almost part of him. How to stand or aim, what to do — he hadn't had to think of it. And he'd never forget the feeling that ran through his body, the sound at impact as that very first ball flew away with the crack of a gunshot. Nor, a week later, once Ski had introduced him down at Pointe Park, did the rest of the Renegade Golfers. Beside Ski and Onions that day there was Mad Dog, Screamer, Big John, The German… And they all just stood there, gawping like knuckleheads, mouths hanging open.

'Sheeeet, man!' Onions let out a whoop. 'The kid fuckin' *nailed* it! Did you hear the *strike* on that thing?'

So that's what they called him, from that moment on. It was part of the deal, Ski insisted — they all had their game-tag, *nom de* something, he called it, some bull about

37

warriors and battle. When he was with them, their tight little gang of golf anarchists, it was goodbye to Rico, the whip-thin punk from Allapattah who nobody noticed, and hello to wonderboy.

'Strike?—That's just perfect, man. You've no idea . . .' Ski nearly wet himself laughing. He and Onions high-fived. 'I tell you, this guy and work, they don't mix. Ain't that right, kid?'

Even Rico had to smile. Office clerk, cleaner, retail assistant . . . he'd never stayed anyplace long. OK, time-keeping wasn't his strength. And not long after this, meeting Ski and the others, he'd quit his latest job at the beach. Renting out loungers, parasols, towels. Wherever you were, after a while it was deadsville, you'd just had enough. So he'd faced up to Gilpin, that asshole, and thrown in the towel. Literally. That had felt good. It always did in the moment, telling some guy where to shove it. Till an hour or so later, at least. Till you saw you were back where you started, only worse. No beans and one fewer option.

'Shit, that used to be me,' Ski had told him. 'Hot-headed? Shoulda seen me, man. No sense at all. Was my way or nothin' . . .'

Rico wondered now if any of this would've hap-pened—had he not been on duty that late-afternoon by the shore. Watching from a distance as the latest model-shoot finished. Up near the dunes two girls were back in their wraps, sashaying barefoot away through the sand to the Art Deco promenade, their suites at the Colony, the Avalon. Then this other guy in his swim-trunks—older but toned, he seemed to know the whole crew—had given them a wave and come strolling on down to where Rico was patrolling the chairs, handing out ticket stubs.

The guy paid his three dollars, sank onto a lounger.

Slathered more oil on his chest. He was several shades darker than Rico already. The sun was dropping fast over Ocean Drive, rolling its shadows toward them; maybe half-an-hour more and his shift would be through. He'd just checked his area, there were few bathers left, so he'd lingered while they both looked out at the water. Three or four kids in the shallows were tossing a beach-ball between them.

'How much they pay you for this?' the guy asked.

'Not enough,' he'd shrugged. 'Beats the factories, I guess.'

'Not exactly stretching you either. Huh, kid?'

'Look, man — you want to hustle me, you got the wrong guy.'

The man laid down his sun-oil and smiled.

'Take it easy, kid — we're just talking here, right?' He held out his hand. 'Danny Pawolski.'

'Rico. Rico de Silva.' They shook.

'You don't like the sun, Rico?'

'Oh, er . . . this.' He pulled off the blue canvas hat and looked at it self-consciously. Tugged at the long-sleeved shirt, eased down its cuffs. 'My old man . . . it, like, fucked with his skin. You know? Anyways, he died.'

Rico kept watching the kids with the ball, afraid to catch the man's eye. Neither statement was true. His father had left before Rico was born, was remarried now and back in San Juan. Nor, as far as he knew, had his father's health ever troubled him. The still-livid scars that marked his own wrists, however, bore only one explanation. And that, as he'd discovered too often, either drove people from him or opened up places he'd no wish to revisit. It was simpler to ensure that nobody saw the marks, ever.

'Shit, Rico, I'm sorry. Listen, what else you do? When you're not saving boneheads like me with your parasols.'

39

Most likely he'd shrugged again. Who cares? he thought. Why the fuck do you?

'Hang out,' he replied. 'Watch the bladers, the models. Usual stuff.'

'How about sports? You into the Marlins, the Heat? You gotta skateboard, right?'

'Whatever. Watchin' maybe.'

'Ok, listen. You're hard, you're tough—I got it, OK? So let's quit playing hardball. When you're done here I'll buy you a beer. There's this real cool game I gotta tell you about. Who knows?—you just might enjoy it. Hear me out, kid, at least. See what you think . . .'

Apart from the three Miller Lites, God knows how Ski had persuaded him. All he'd got was a load of psycho-babble, big words, no mention of what this game was. Still, next day he was there, lined up with these twenty-odd kids, all kinds of ages, on some beat-up field near the airport. Half-erased markings, mini-baseball, peeked here and there through the dead grass and dust. Deep shadow covered most of the field from the criss-cross of freeways above them. The whirr of traffic was constant.

'Nah...no way . . .' Ski had popped the trunk of his beat-up Datsun, was pulling out a sack of old clubs. '*Golf*? You're kiddin' me, man. You think this is *cool*?'

'Stay with me, tough guy. Patience, OK? — then maybe we'll get there.'

Ski was one of the coaches. Tossed him this thing with an 8 on the bottom. Rico stood and swished it back and forth for a while, no sign of a ball, as a stubby little bald guy, belly hanging over his pants, stood out front yelling instructions, showing them the moves, while Ski and another two guys worked the line. Rico stood off to one end and paid no attention, thinking what a dumb-ass he'd been, praying no one he knew got to hear of this. All the same, the club felt good in his hands, comfortable there, kinda powerful — *swish-swish* — and at length he found nine or ten balls being tipped at his feet.

'Ok, fellas, time to try it for real . . .'

After a couple of whiffs, missing the darn thing completely, he felt his third swing make contact. The ball flew away with a satisfying *zing*. He had no idea how, or where it had gone. And then he looked up. The ball was still rising as it cleared the mesh fence at the end of the field and clattered, audibly, into something metallic on the far side. He glanced across nervously. The whole line had stopped swinging, was staring across at him. And all four coaches were heading his way, jaws set, scowls on their faces.

'D'ya see that?' said the tallest, a big-shouldered black guy with tight steely hair.

'Yeah, Vern,' answered another, looking back to where the shot had headed. 'I sure did. Heard it too.'

'What's your name, kid?' asked Baldie as they reached him.

'His name's Rico,' Ski told them.

'How old are you, Rico?'

'Nineteen.'

'Well, kid, this here's a class for beginner's. You can see that, huh?' Baldie lifted the iron he was holding, pointed its shaft down the row of faces, all drifting closer. 'You had your fun. Now gimme that club and sciddadle. Go on, get the hell outa here.'

'Take it easy, Frank.' Ski took a step forward. 'I brought him. He didn't want to be here, believe me. And he's not held a club till today.'

'That true, kid?'

Rico nodded.

The black dude, Vern, whistled through his teeth. 'Tell

you what, Rico. How about you show us that swing again, huh? Looked pretty damn mean from where I stood.'

So he did. Hit four or five more while they all looked on. Three balls followed the first, the other two just failed to make it, hitting the fence on the fly.

Vern stood scratching his head. Baldie Frank stroked his moustache. No one said nothing. Rico didn't know what to make of it either. How was he supposed to hit it? Were they pleased or still mad? He stood there ducking his head, shifting from foot to foot, hating the focus upon him.

'Can't say where you found him, baby,' it was Vern who broke the silence, 'but reckon this here's a natural . . .'

As Rico glanced up Ski caught his eye, gave a wink.

'Well, boys,' he said. 'Whaddya know? How cool is that?'

❧

Later, early evening, heat just beginning to ease, they dropped by Ted's Hideaway for two or three glasses then walked up the block to Ski's place on 4th.

That was when he first raised the subject of street golf. A way ordinary guys like the two of them, without country-club wallets or even public course dress-codes, could enjoy the great game. Over the years a small group had evolved called The Renegades. They made up their own rules and tee-times: put the quiet moonlit beaches and jetties, vacant lots, auto graveyards to alternate use.

'We're still the hardcore,' said Ski, reaching his door. 'The game at its purest. You seen that new store up on Drexel? — Punk Golf or something? Puh, you just gotta look at the place. Load of pussies. Trying to cash in, pimp it up with designer gear, beach parties, all kindsa shit. Even play with this special soft ball. Fuckin' sell-outs, man. All they're after's a villa and pool out in Pinecrest . . .'

His home was one airless room, cluttered with dumb-bells, diving gear, heaps of old junk. Ski threw off his shirt, flicked on the overhead fan, propped the door open onto the street. Fetching them another two Buds from the ice-box he dropped stiffly into a moth-eaten armchair, sweat glistening on his chest.

'Man oh man' he murmured, rolling the chilled bottle over his brow. 'You want the real thing, a true rush . . . you stick with the Renegades.'

He reached down and winced, scooped up a small plastic jar. Shook out two or three tablets, knocked them back with a drinker's deep pull on the bottle.

'Never mind me,' his smile was more of a grimace. 'Should've treated this body way kinder. Taken too many hits down the years . . .'

'Percocet, right?'

Ski paused, the bottle halfway to his lips. 'What, you a doctor now, Rico? What the fuck do you know?'

'You tried Demerol? Tylox? Way better for pain. Two to one with some Ambien. You'll be floatin' '.

Ski looked at him. Shook his head and chuckled. 'You're something else, kid—you know that?'

He took another swig, aimed the remote. Some soft-porn movie flickered into life in the corner, sound lowered. Outside the light was fading fast. They sat there a while in the wavering blue, eyes glazing over, vacantly watching . . .

Rico had tried not to think of it, not in years—how he knew what he did. But Ski's look, his unanswered question, took him back to the reek of oil and exhaust fumes; his bed in that little back-room. He'd be five, six years old at the most. Out back and next door was Haley's, the largest auto service uptown. The nine-to-five screeching of air-hoses; engines gunned and retuned; hub-caps spinning and falling; the drilling and grinding. Its fumes were part of the neighbourhood: curtains, sofas and beds, the flimsy wallpapered walls — you couldn't scrub or spray them away any more than seal out the noise. For years he took the headaches for granted. But this particular time, what he remembered was coughing and coughing. Mom spooning that syrup into his throat. Even now, it seemed, he could smell the cherry-black linctus, savour each spoonful again, how swiftly and often that bottle had calmed or revived him, come to his aid.

And later, lost in the hell that was High School, all the shit that came with it — how the urge had first seized him to search through the cupboards, find something that offered a similar kindness. He'd waited for a night when Celestina and Vincent were out on their latest hot dates, his mom safely sleeping upstairs, then started hunting. By then she was already diagnosed, on a diet of so many pills he'd lost count, so that what he discovered — laying out capsules and tablets in rows on the sideboard, so many sizes and colours — looked like a candy store . . .

'Here you go, champ. Take a hit.'

Ski had lit up a joint. Rico took a couple of tokes, drew the smoke in deep, passed the roach back.

Back then he'd had no idea what each drug was for, which of her symptoms they eased or suppressed. All he knew, and by heart, were combinations and doses — at least for a woman of fifty with inoperable tumours, the shrinking body and weight of a child — since it often fell to him to check and administer. For all that — in a welter of shame and self-loathing — that first time he'd just closed his eyes, swallowed several at random. Then sat at the table, watched its old oilskin cover start dancing. If they could smother and deaden her pain, why not his? He was as angry, terrified, exhausted of watching her wither and die, day by slow day, as she was enduring it. To hear her stifled, gut-wrenching moans through the clapboard partitions. He was sick of his own life, too; her illness had helped him discover this. Sick of riding the trash-carts, sweeping streets, then the bedpans and buckets at home.

But the pills, at least, helped him to a different place. The next day in class he seemed to glide right through it. As though, overnight, he'd been rendered invisible. Later that week he palmed a few more, another rainbow selection, carried them to school in his pocket. More than one kid in his class — Connor Brown, Mitch Adams for sure — he knew were on some kind of tablet just to keep them in line. Miss a dose and they never kept still, would act like they should be in Grade School. Mitch even took out his jang once, fired a high golden arc across four or five desks. Hit Greta Saul's hair like a bull's-eye. Even now he could hear Greta scream; see himself sitting there, grinning like hell as the chaos ensued...

And a day or two later he got somewhere quiet with the Ritalin twins. Bartered the first of his own little stash for theirs. The rest, as they say, was history. His history. Ritalin, OxyContin, Percocet, Valium, Xanax, Dexedrine. No wonder, by the time he skipped school, he was known as the Pharmacy Kid.

He and Ski headed off, this time wordlessly, up the 5th fairway. He toward the glitter of lake, the dogleg's corner, Ski soon but a vanishing shadow away to his right, lost against the trees.

Strike expected his ball to be sitting up nicely, clearly visible from within a few yards. Close to the corner, maybe just past it. Reaching there, he searched a small circle of fairway for a minute or so, but saw nothing. He could just make Ski out, some distance off in the tree-line opposite, still searching himself.

Fuck it, he murmured, swishing the club back and forth. *Come on, come on . . .* Despite his stash of balls he hated to lose even one. Even more, to give Ski an opening, take a two-shot penalty. *Oh, man.* On a reflex he fished another tab from his shirt. He was levelling out, needed to keep the rush going. And they helped his night vision. He moved through the low semi-rough, on down a slight slope to the edge of the rushes. They towered well above him, pale as ghosts, very still. The frogs were really partying here. Even the sound of them was dirty as hell. A narrow, trampled-flat path led away to the door of the pumphouse, a big silver padlock glinting on its catch.

Without warning the same call as earlier—a dry lonely note, maybe a heron—sounded just to his left. He felt his heart jump in its cage, a surge of heat shooting through him. As if in response something rustled in the reeds near his feet, followed by audible moan. Strike stood there, still as a fox. The sound came again, clearer this time. Peering toward it he took a single small step and pitched straight over. The club flew out of his hand.

'Jesus . . . what the . . .?'

Smelling sweat and cheap wine, he tried to pull himself up. Something was moving beside him. On its hands and knees. What he'd taken at first for a stray piece of timber—a bunker tie perhaps, stored out of sight by the green-staff—he saw now was somebody's leg. The figure was mumbling to itself and then retching, barely sober enough to drag its own weight, trying to crawl off into the rushes. Like another, almost physical blow, Strike caught the stench of fresh vomit.

Back on his feet, he glanced around for the club. Couldn't see it. But the upper was kicking in fast. He felt his face start to tighten, contract. Stars sparkled overhead, the hollow glowed with tatters of fog.

'Hey, hombre.' He tried not to giggle. 'You crazy or what. . .? The hell you doing out here?'

But the guy was way gone, clearly some wino who'd mislaid his compass. Strike thought about leaving him to it, resuming his search—but, hey, what the hell, this was all pretty wild and the fella intrigued him now. To make it to here, never mind in his state, took some doing. Gave them something in common.

He looked back at the pumphouse, just a few yards away. It wouldn't take a moment to prop him up there, let him sleep it off in a little more comfort. Standing astride the guy's back he bent forward, nearly puking himself from the sour-sweet smell. Got a hold under his arms and lifted.

'Whavvalo . . . gerra-shay . . .' the guy muttered, head lolling. His long matted hair was a veil.

He wasn't big but every ounce was dead weight. Strike half-dragged, half-lifted him out from behind. It was only four or five yards to the pumphouse wall. He tried to lean him against it but the long skinny head, it's mop of rank hair, kept lolling over while the fool kept on with his mumbling.

'OK, joe. You take care now. Nice little caddy-shack, huh? Your own sweet motel.'

Strike put out a hand, tried to ease his head upright. 'Hey, you play golf?' The laughter bubbled out of him now. 'Next time you can join us for nine. What ya say?'

He still hadn't seen the guy clearly. Easing aside the

curtain of hair he looked into a gaunt, bony face, sunken shadows for cheeks, cloudy unfocused eyes that rolled in their sockets like a blind man's. But all Strike could focus on was the swelling that bulged from his forehead, the deep gash at its centre. And the stickiness in his own hands. He held them up where he could see. The blood appeared black on his fingers, glistening like oil.

'Jesus . . .. oh, man . . .' He let go, took a step back. Stared at the dark-coated figure, slumped against the whitewash like someone just shot. Then he was scrambling away up the bank. Almost straight into Ski.

'Hey, pro . . . you just missed a ripper. Must be right up there . . .' He turned back to Strike from the imagined green, two-fifty ahead. Peered past him into the reeds. Gave a low chuckle. 'Don't tell me you lost it. Down there?—Shit, champ, I may fuckin' have you at last . . .'

Strike tried to keep his hands low, wiped them on his pants. Time seemed to have stopped. Words wouldn't come. He was telling himself most of the bums back in town looked no better. Fights and falls came with the territory. The fool could have tripped just like he had; or been whacked somewhere else, for a mattress or bottle. Maybe he'd stumbled out here to escape something worse.

'Yeah... I mean, no. Must be there somewhere. There's this . . .. there's some guy . . . I dunno.' He paused, touched his temple. Pulled his hand quickly down, afraid Ski would notice. Everything was spinning. He felt like his skull was about to explode. 'I mean . . . what the hell's he doing there anyhow?'

Ski stared at him blankly. 'That blood?' he asked, nodding. Then a faint smile broke. 'You're fuckin' stoned, man.' He put a hand on Strike's shoulder. 'Wait here, I'll go take a look.' And he vanished from sight down the bank.

Strike couldn't wait, his legs were already moving. He was sweating real bad now, his shirt felt glued on. He hurried back across the fairway, where Ski had come from. Through the trees he could make out the glow of the city, the beltway's lights. He headed straight for them, fast as he could.

After maybe a minute he heard Ski behind him. Running, catching him up. 'Hey, where you going . . .' This time the hand tried pulling him back, but Strike kept on walking.

'Now wait a minute, junior!'

Ski jumped in front of him, breathing hard in his face, forcing him to stop.

'We got holes still to play here, remember? Lose one lousy ball and you walk off the course? Uh-uh,' he wagged a finger, gave a choked, bitter laugh. 'Those aint the rules. I got you by the *cojones*, kid. First time in months.'

The black pools of his eyes held a sharp little glimmer. Strike could make out the cords in Ski's neck, flexing and tensing. His jaw too. *Shit*, he thought, *here we go*, and cursed himself again. For letting Ski talk him into it, for believing what he said—that the business between them was buried. You only had to look at him now to know that was bull.

'Forget this, did you champ?' Ski held up the club and lobbed it across. Strike caught it. 'What's got into you, huh? Spot of blood spooked you? C'mon, for Chrissake. Drop one and rip it. We've a game to finish . . . '

Strike could only stare dumbly. He wanted to believe Ski was kidding but knew from his tone, his glittering stare, that he wasn't. The guy was still up in orbit while he was coming down fast.

'You've fuckin' lost it. You're nuts.' He rubbed a hand over his face, hoping the whole night would vanish. 'You

seen the guy. We need to be outa here. Now.' He shoved
Ski aside.

'Hey, take it easy. Let him sleep the thing off, he'll be
fine. These guys are tough, man, you know it.' He looked
back at the reeds. 'You weren't kidding, he took a good
hit. But it's done,' he shrugged. 'No more we can do.'

'You're fuckin' serious. You are. You want to play on.'

'Sure. Why not? Why the fuck wouldn't I? Why
wouldn't *you*?' He shook his head, laughed again bitterly.
'Oh, I get it. Think you're the only winner round here.
Losing something that matters — it aint such a party now,
right?'

Strike knew perfectly well, they both did, what he was
talking about. And it sure wasn't golf.

He took a last look at Ski's face — this was what fury,
resentment, the churning of envy must look like, up
close — then pushed his way past.

'You're fuckin' sick, man. I'm outa here. Play on if
you like . . .'

He took a few paces, broke into a jog, kept going. At
last he'd said something worthwhile. It felt pretty good.
Ski was still calling after him. . . .

'. . . unfinished business here, kid . . . this game it aint
over . . . you better believe it . . .'

. . .but it made no difference. Whether from nerves or
adrenalin, maybe the candy, he was glowing inside. And
Ski's voice had soon faded, drowned out by the whoosh-
ing of traffic.

Strike kept on going, on toward the lights and the
sound.

Ski was right about one thing, of course. He'd seen Julie
first. No argument there.

Fresh in from Ohio with a college friend, Vicky, she'd just landed this waitressing job at News Café. The News was prime territory, an Ocean Drive fixture; favoured hang-out of writers, producers, agency scouts. For every wannabe model and actor, working the bar and the side-walk tables was their showcase and runway, the chance to impress the contacts they needed. The whole ocean front might be wall-to-wall chic, boutiques and hotels — but The News hired the best-looking staff, everyone knew it. And once he'd seen Julie, Rico didn't doubt her appear-ance had swung her the job. The funny part was, as he discovered, Julie didn't care about movies or modelling. What had led her to here were the winters back in Defi-ance, her longing to see other places, dive some reefs while she saved for a course in marine conservation.

So, there she was, finding her feet in South Beach, closing down her third shift at The News — wiping tables, scooping up tips — when she and Ski had got talking.

He'd appeared near the end of the evening, she said. At News prices, Rico knew he'd only be there to eye up the tootsie; make a glass or two last until closing then hope to hit lucky.

'I dunno . . . he's a nice enough guy, charming really. Done some real crazy things, worked interesting places — you know that . . .'

That was true also. By then Rico had known him for close to six months. Not long before, with his movie work dying, Ski had managed to fast-talk himself into two days a week at the Surf & Dive Center close to the beach. Perry and Dan and the others — they majored on surfing, could sell a body- or skim-board to anyone — but Ski had been a diver in his day, deep below the rigs, some-where off of Holland or England. (*'Tellin' ya, kid — you can't make or keep a darn thing without risk. Nothing worth having, at least. Learned that pretty fast. You could say I been diving—leaping and diving—every day since . . .'*) And he'd told Rico how, back on one of the bad days, his tank had run low. How they'd hauled him up too fucking fast and those bubbles of air had pretty near killed him...

Rico could picture it—Ski spinning it all out again to Julie that night. Big winning smile, shirt open just far enough. Jeans and tooled boots, his better leg crossed casually over the other as if he was still the star quarterback. Telling her how, after that, his fitness and muscle were shot, how stiffness and pain set up house in his tendons and joints. (*'Passed out twenty-five, woke up forty—that's how it was. Somedays now I'm just wood glued together'*). And how it took Florida, its wet oily heat—a self-imposed diet and months at the gym—to get back in shape.

Course, one thing he may not have mentioned to Julie were the doc's little tablets. *But that's where it started,* Ski had confessed to him. The craving, dependence, the regular fix. *Couldn't eat, move or piss straight without them. Fentanyl, Darvon, Vicodin. It's those little babies got me back on my feet.* Found new buyers for his Action Man skills—directors, movie crews, ad-men; kept him afloat for a while. But now here he was, treading water or worse, watching the store every Thursday. Pushing dive-suits and regulators, deepwater watches. Helping out Sundays with dive-school tuition, down at the 3rd Street break.

'Well, I wasn't seeing anyone,' Julie continued, 'not since back home. So when he asked me . . . yeah, it was kind of exciting. And don't get me wrong, next night we got on just fine. Ate at Van Dyke's then stayed for the show, it was nice . . .'

'But you just kinda knew, huh?'

'I guess. Not to get serious with anyway. We were talking, but not the same things. Probably an age thing—you know how it is—but I just couldn't tell him, not then. And anyhow, I didn't think it would matter, I thought he understood . . .'

Huh! As if. And they knew it real soon.

Rico's next free day, in fact. Mid-afternoon. He'd just stepped out of the Smoke Shop with a four-dollar bag of tobacco when, a distance away, he caught sight of Ski's back, his slick of grey-black hair, unmistakeable Hawaiian shirt. He was sitting on the low sea wall, half turned away, and it wasn't till he got close that Rico even noticed the girl he was talking with. But hell, then he did. The shock of short choppy hair, white as a fresh fall of snow. And the eyes, peeking out from that fringe, an awesome grey-green. Killer smile, cheekbones, long elfin face. He hadn't been able to focus on what she was saying, just the way she was smiling, moving her hands as she spoke. In her frayed cut-off shorts she was skinny as him, all arms and legs and much the same height—but a whole lot cuter. An electric charge surged right through him, before she or Ski had even looked up.

Once they did he had to fight to stay cool, try not to gawp at her like some tenth-grade geek.

'Hey, how's it goin'?' Ski was all smiles, wrapped an arm round his back.

'Look at that,' he turned to the girl, 'I just mention the guy, next thing he's stood here! Meet the wonderkid, baby. Rico—aka Striker or Strike. And this vision here's Julie . . .'

Rico nodded, half-smiled, looked to the ground. Far as he could tell, she did the same.

It seemed like forever then, him hanging there—tugging

his sleeves, shoving hands in his baggies, rolling a cigarette—as the two of them talked. But it was maybe just
a minute or so. And then it struck him that just Ski was
speaking—still about their Renegade gang—so he drew
in some smoke, snuck another look at the girl. Ski had
sat himself back on the wall, half facing Julie, while Rico
stood off just behind him. So when he looked up, caught
her glancing at him with another faint smile, it shook him
to his bones. Was he certain? He had to be seeing things,
surely? At least Ski—spouting some poem now—didn't
appear to have noticed.

'Honey, I'm serious,' she said as they lay in her room
the following weekend. Vicky had headed downtown to
check out some gallery, they had the place to themselves.
'I was real real glad you showed up. Took the pressure
right off . . . well, until . . .'

'Yeah, right,' Strike smiled, recalling each second.
How it soon became clear he hadn't imagined it. That
Ski must've read from her wavering eyes (maybe one
glance too many) that her attention was elsewhere. In
any case, all at once he'd stopped talking, had turned and
was staring at him, then at Julie. Blankly at first, back and
forth, as if—like Rico himself—he couldn't quite take
it in. *Oh yeah.* Ski thought. *That was the moment. That did
it for sure.*

And OK, it was tough on him. But things happen,
and Ski was tough too. They'd not planned it this way
after all. Like Julie, Rico assumed he'd get over it. A
week, maybe two, the old dog would be fine, happy for
them even, and things would go on as before. But it soon
became clear—in his glares and cutting asides, the sudden
absences from which he'd resurface, days later, with the
bleary unshaven look of someone who'd partied too
well—that Ski fallen for Julie real hard. That how he still

saw it, what gnawed at his guts worst of all, was that Rico
had stolen her from him. Had betrayed his friendship, his
openness, whatever bond they had forged.

After that, once he and Julie were dating, Rico saw
little of Ski for some weeks. Once they passed in the
street, another time in the grocery aisle. Exchanged just
a nod, a mumbled acknowledgement. Rico had longed
to say more — try to make Ski see reason, that Julie had
simply expressed where her preference lay — but he could
tell right away that Ski was closed tight as a clam, had no
interest in talking.

It must've been close to a month when, settled in at
the Deuce Bar one night, Ski brushed by his table heading
into the john. This time Rico was sure he'd not seen him.
He toyed with it a moment then followed him in, closed
the door, leaned against it.

'Look, this is just crazy . . .'

Ski was the only one there, standing at one of the stalls.
He glanced Rico's way, registered an instant's surprise,
then looked down again, shaking his head.

'Well? You don't think it's time?' Rico continued. 'To
draw a line under this? Man, I don't know you no more.
But I want to, OK? There, I said it. And I'm sorry, right.
For how it's turned out . . .'

He couldn't say it made a whole lot of difference. Ski
simply zipped up, rinsed off his hands and catching Rico's
eye in the mirror, muttered something like: *figure for the
time of scorn* . . . And with a weird smile, a look that made
Rico step to one side — returned to the bar.

What the hell. What kind of cartwheels was the old
guy on? But at least Rico knew that he'd heard it. And
after that evening, though the looks were still there, the
edgy silences, more wacko quotes — at least, soon after
that, he and the Renegades began to see more of him,

he'd join them for a game now and then. And little by little — through glances, grudging acknowledgement for each other's shots, a beer bought, a jay rolled and shared — it seemed an unspoken truce was established them.

It had been one crazy summer.

The winter hurricane had barely blown through, the clean-up still underway, when the heatwave arrived, settled like a blanket across the whole state. Ice factories, air-conditioning plants, even the emergency wards — nothing could cope with it. Old folks were dropping like flies from the heatstroke.

For a while there, Rico had two jobs part-time — working the store-room at Publix, stacking shelves in the Alton Road 7-Eleven. Other times he spent tanking up, cooling down, getting high again. Only way to get through it. Some nights one or more of the gang would meet up, head off wherever chance carried them. Find an unpatrolled depot, back alley; pick a route, their first target, head out. Most times they were savvy enough to stay ahead of the cops; knew every exit, had their bail-outs planned. Even so, some rounds finished early to lights coming on, cursing and protest, sirens screaming as they hightailed it. One time in the early hours they snuck into a boarded-up, once-grand hotel right on Ocean; found four or five bums who were camped there, real cosy in the echoing, still ornate lobby. The guys had their cans, had rigged up a fucking TV for Chrissake. Were so glued to some *Dynasty* re-run they raised barely a murmur as he and the others slipped by. Via the service stairs they'd found their juice- and mojo-fuelled way to an awesome,

open-air rooftop, slugged a few balls out at the now dark-
ened sand, the phosphorescent breakers.

Another night he and Ski ended up in a library-like
room at the Hotel Cabana, right on the beach. Through
the door at the back you could hear the breakers thud in,
suck out, roll in again. The event was some kind of poetry
thing. All manner of screwballs appeared unannounced,
wandered in and out, sat and listened, got up and spouted
their nonsense. Some guy who called himself Simca, long
frizzy beard, looked like a Rabbi. A flame-haired stripper,
already wasted, giggling non-stop where she'd crashed on
some cushions. And the host himself, a real straight college
kid who made a big deal of announcing each act. Rico
knew Ski wouldn't be there unless he meant to take part.
Jeez, if he couldn't make use of words here, where could
he? Sure enough, when his turn came he started waving
his hands, talking in some weird foreign language (Rico
wasn't sure if it was Russian or French) translating each
line as he went:

'. . . *ooh la-la, Napoleon really fucked Russia up and now
Chirac's done it to Belleville—*

*slick suits aren't our ruin, my darlings, it's the workers that
refuse to revolt . . .*

*what we need is an army of those small green machines, each
one a genius,*

cruising our sidewalks, hoovering the shit . . .'

Anyhow, that's what it sounded like. Rico didn't
understand diddly but near killed himself laughing. So
did most of the room, which sent frat boy right over the
edge. He made them leave after that. Looking back, this
was maybe the night that Rico felt closest to Ski, not just
in awe of him but believing they'd always be close. The
guy kept surprising him, seemed to live every moment
with a fierce kind of passion, things that Rico still aspired

to and envied. Rolling out of Cabana together, he felt near to happiness and knew it was Ski who was largely responsible. It didn't seem possible that things could ever be different.

And these were the months of the Monkey Knife Fight. Whatever this was, it was said to have started in South Beach; but soon, like the heat, it covered the city. Spray-painted stencils on pavements, fences and walls. Little stickers in restrooms, on tills at the checkout. It all set the tone for the sweltering summer, became somehow its emblem, the chant on everyone's lips. Because no one knew what it meant or who lay behind it there were all kinds of theory and rumour. Some claimed it was a gang thing, others a band trying to whip up PR. People stopped on the street to discuss it. First The Herald then the Times ran special features. But all they had was hot air, more speculation. And the three words they started with.

'Shit, man, it's a joke, can't they see?' Ski was adamant, brushed the whole thing aside. 'It means nothing, there's no fucking answer. That's just the point, right?'

Rico had to come down, had to think.

Around ten pm he dropped another Seconal, knocked it back with a hit of warm Coors then went outside on the step. Closing the screen door behind him his fingers jumped from the latch as a tingle of current went through him.

Nights like this—humidity in the 90's, scarce able to breathe—an odd stillness came over the place. Like the charge in the air had been sucked from the people, they had no fight or energy left, were now simply waiting for something. Maybe just a storm, a few cooler hours. He rolled a straight cigarette; lit up and drew in the smoke.

All at once, sitting there, everything took on a new clarity. He watched the smoke drift, rise through the patches of light, vanish overhead. Seemed to follow it up there, was able to see the whole neighbourhood, the grid of streets he'd know blindfold. Look, the guys were still there, rooting through dumpsters outside the station, curled in its doorways. Just over the rooftops, the cause-way, Ferraris, Corvettes, Maseratis gleamed at the curb-side like maybugs. Then the surf — one pure line in the dark. And back here his neighbourhood, this very street. He saw how the light from each room, his own shadow, lay out in the road. Doors and windows stood open, he could hear murmured voices, the clink of dishes and pans, laughter from a nearby room. Smell the kitchen of Lara Rodriguez, her great *bacalaítos* . . .

On nights such as this he was glad that he lived here, despite all the shit. Sure, he once had had his dreams, just like anyone else. Mansions in Hialeah, Key Biscayne. Sweeping up the drive between manicured, sprinkler-wet lawns in his red Lamborghini; braking in a spray of gravel by some big white columns. Skipping inside to the super-hot babe who awaited him.

But who was he kidding? This was where he belonged, always would. Like Ski had said, who wanted that closed-down, predictable life behind fences and gates? Who knows, maybe he'd find it now anyway — in the Metro West cellblocks or at TGK.

The cops, two patrolmen, had come to his door just this morning. Tried to keep it real casual, just a few ques-tions. Word on the street was that Rico had taken up golf, had some clubs — even took them out *nights*? Now why would that be? How about Tuesday? Ever been near

Bayshore? This drifter had taken some beating, five or six blows, the docs reckoned a golf club. Touch and go if he'd make it. Rico was happy to help, right? Wouldn't mind if they borrowed those clubs for a while, ran a few tests . . .?

What could he say? But well before they left the whole picture hit him. They knew way too much, and too soon. And only one guy could have told them, sent them his way. The guy he'd never known after all. Who'd seen the blood on his hands, his clothes; gone into that hollow then found his club lying there too, like a gift. In one fucked-up moment, the chance to win all he wanted . . .

Rico watched Kayla and Luis stroll by, arm in arm. Obie Bermúdez, 'Ya Te Olvide,' was playing on a radio upstairs. Here, for just a while longer, was comfort, security, among his own kind. Where his mother had born, raised and nursed him till he had nursed her. Watched her wither and shrink back to bone. And now she was out there as well, with so many others, where the waters were gathering. Allapattah. Place of the alligator. That's what the Seminoles called it. And these were the nights, in the thick heavy air, you could still smell the swamp. Just beneath the concrete and steel, its thin human crust. Vaporous, fetid, full of eager decay.

It wasn't just Ski's word and his. Whatever they found on that 5-iron — traces down in the grooves, his prints alone on the grip (Ski had his glove on as always) — the lab stuff would all point to him. If it wasn't so sick, it was perfect. They'd be back for him soon, and his clothes. Wherever Ski was, he must feel pretty swell. And if the hobo checked out — well, wonderkid really was history. Out of his way, his and Julie's, for good.

Rico stubbed out the cigarette, drained the last of the can. Hugged himself as he sat there, shivering suddenly in spite of the heat. It was clear to him now that the snakes and the gators, the insects themselves, all of the predators had simply retreated. Into the tree-lines, the mangroves and Everglades, the underground rivers and pools. Surrounding the city, they waited. Waited and watched for the creatures—careless and smug, quite unprepared—to lower their guard. Ready to reclaim what was theirs.

Meanwhile, he thought, all you could do was hold on. To whatever it was that you had.

Even that wasn't easy.

Tajine with Madonna

THEY CALL MOHKRAN an oasis, but to her it seemed like a dead place.

Eve shielded her face from the spiraling sand as the jeep drew away. Even through her dark glasses the alley was pink in the dusk. Bending forward she picked up her bags from where the driver had dumped them. He'd muttered something in French that sounded like *Pension Jereed*, then with a sigh spelt it out: D-J-E-R-I-D.

Presumably he'd stopped somewhere near, though from the unbroken mud-red walls that rose on each side of her, there was no means of telling. And no one to ask: the narrow street was deserted.

Then, just along it, she noticed someone: a diminutive, white-robed man, his face very dark. Leaning casually in a doorway, he examined her fixedly. Sudanese, she told herself, walking forward. Even this small observation helped ease her headache, reassured her that for this assignment her research had been thorough.

In fact, she saw now, the man was not small. The entrance where he stood was two steps down from the street. The deep shadow behind him made her think of a burrow dug in the sand. From it came the oily smell of meat cooking. Somewhere a sheep bleated mournfully in the dry, still air.

'*Pardon, m'sieur. Je cherche . . .*'

A sharp human cry cut her short. She turned, heard

a series of yelps and squeals. Through the fiery veil, still
suspended where her taxi had been, a pack of small children came hurtling toward her, waving and shrieking.
Before she had time to react she felt a tug on her arms,
looked back to see yet another infant—a barefooted boy
with blue-black hair shorn close to his skull—hurrying
through an arch which lay opposite. Her two bags swayed
beside him, almost dragging the dirt. To keep sight of her
things and escape the oncoming hoard she pursued the
child without thought. At the end of a passageway she
spotted him, holding open a thick wooden door. Reinforced with black studs, a small grille at eye-level, it was
like entering a prison. The door closed behind her and she
heard a bolt drawn across.

Facing them was a small enclosed courtyard. A bright
yellow towel hung drying from a window above. As on
the street the inner walls were of dull reddish clay, pitted
and crumbling. The boy looked her up and down with
his enormous dark eyes then grunted something. It meant
nothing to her. She began climbing after him, up a flight
of steep narrow steps which twisted into the gloom.

They emerged on a gallery. The only light came from
a little square of sky; beneath it, in another yard, she made
out some duckboards, heard the faint gurgling of water.
They passed one door before the boy stopped. The size
of key he pushed into the lock reinforced her impression
of dungeons. Below, as she followed him in, she thought
she heard someone walking: bare feet slapping rhythmi-
cally over wet stone.

The boy set down the bags, went across and pushed
wider a small creaking shutter. She looked about her,
appalled. There was no space to move and the ceiling
was barely a foot from her head. A low narrow board
ran the length of one wall; she wouldn't have recognised

it as a bed had not the blanket been lying there. Ragged and crumpled — as though the last occupant had only a moment ago thrown it off — she stared at it with disgust. The boy struck a match, applied it to a battered-looking lamp which began to burn smokily. At the foot of the bed on a low, three-legged *taifor* was a pitcher of water in an earthenware bowl.

Edging by, she stood at the window. It overlooked the first, larger yard. Several other windows opened onto it: leaning further she saw that the one with the yellow towel was next door. She turned back and found the kid grinning vacantly up at her.

'*Et le tarif?*' she asked. She could feel the grit through the soles of her thin canvas shoes; sense it piled in the corners which the flickering light didn't touch. '*Deux nuits . . . trois, peut-être.*'

'*Ah, oui,*' smiling in response, amused by her pronunciation. 'You are American?' he continued in English.

She nodded, sighing. 'But how much.'

'Thirty dollar. Two day.' His grin never wavered.

'*Thirty?* You're kidding!' She made a move for the bags. 'I'll find someplace else.'

'No else,' he beamed. 'Only *fondouk* for camel.'

Fumbling in her shoulder-sack — a big leather *choukhara* she'd bought in Algiers — she gave him the change from her taxi. As a tip it was excessive but she wished him gone.

To put as much distance as possible between herself and the ceiling she yanked off the blanket and lay down, hands pillowing her head. The board bit at once at each vertebra. She was never going to sleep on this thing.

If the purpose of Larcum's withdrawal here had been to discourage visitors, she imagined it had proved a success. Now she saw what a hole Mohkran was, she found it harder than ever to picture how he was living. Christ, to throw up Europe, that hilltop retreat in Ibiza — for *this*! There had to be easier ways to achieve anonymity.

Now that she was still the familiar throbbing returned, deep behind her eyes. She realised she'd eaten nothing since daybreak — a roll and some godawful coffee forced down with the fumes of the bus depot. It occurred to her vaguely that she ought to go out again, trace that hideous aroma back to its source. When she did rise, however, it was only to fish two Nembutal from her bag. The water from the pitcher was brackish and warm. She dropped in some Sterotabs before collapsing once more. Closing her eyes she tried to exclude any thought of the desert around her.

Some time later she awoke. The lamp had gone out and the darkness was cold. Hugging herself tighter she lay still and listened.

Something strange had been howling just now — a jackal? hyena? — or was that part of her dream? For the first time she noticed above her four splinters of moon-light, the outline of a trapdoor. Heavily she turned her head, looking for a way up. There were no steps, she knew that. The wall at her side was rough and irregu-lar, however, and shortly she realised that certain notches were deliberate footholds.

She reached out, groped for her cigarettes and a sweater. Then she stood on the bed and pushed up at the trap. It gave without trouble.

She found herself on a small flat roof with a rampart-like, shoulder-high wall all around. The merest wind stirred. The moon remained, but behind a high dune lay the first sign of dawn, the finest pale thread. The dune itself cast its shadow deep into the town, right to the foot of the wall where she stood. Again she had the impression of a smooth-sided bowl with herself in its basin: all round the rim the sand seemed set to pile over. She took out a cigarette, lit it and inhaled deeply, leaning on the parapet. She felt easier looking down on the empty street, tracing with the red point of ash the fort's silhouette on the escarpment, the ragged outline of palms at its feet, the minaret's needle.

She flicked the stub into the dark. There was none of the coast's humidity here, just a dry electrical stillness. She was certain her migraines were related to this, to the faint but discernible building of pressure. There was also *Id el Adha*, of course — the Great Day, the Sacrifice of the Sheep — just a few days ahead. Preparations for this generated their own form of tension. In Algiers it was impossible to miss the tethered rams in the market; she'd chanced across a whole flock being herded through the passages of the Kasbah; and even here there was the inescapable bleating. Perhaps once blood had been spilt, the first throat cut, her headaches would cease.

The first quavering notes of the *muezzin* sent a host of small birds pinging down from the minaret. She returned to the room, threw some water over her face and dressed quickly: fresh T-shirt, loose chino pants. There was a threshold of tiredness beyond which further sleep was impossible. She'd go out shortly, find a mint tea or something; no point calling on Larcum much before nine. First she sat on the bed, smoked another Lucky Strike, wondering for the umpteenth time about Ed and the letter she must write him.

Sure, she should've told him before this. Face to face. But somehow the right moment had never presented itself. She couldn't think how their engagement had happened or how he'd persuaded her. *Mrs Edward Legree*: the prospect now made her shudder. The past months had been a question of how to escape without seeming the bitch of all times. Ed, perhaps not wholly oblivious, had tried to dissuade her from making the trip. *Damit, honey, it's you and me now. We need to make plans.* She could still hear his tremor of panic. He'd strode the apartment the whole time she was packing. She knew he considered her thoughtless, foolhardy; feared all manner of nebulous danger. And of course it was true: she was conscious that coming after Larcum now might in some way force her hand.

La ilaha . . . illa Allah . . . Mohammed rasul Allah . . . The *muezzin* droned on.

She'd always assumed that to return to New York was inevitable. But what had been keeping her there, beside Ed? Not love for the city, certainly, and the Larcum thing could be handled from anywhere. Syndicated worldwide (as it should be) it would buy all the time she needed. Meanwhile what she needed was shelter, anyplace, long enough to figure things out. Her return flight was via Paris: she could stay there, find a room, get the story in shape. Sure, why not?

Feeling almost lightheaded, she grabbed her bag and went out.

She found breakfast by chance, and closer than expected. A big plain woman — swathed head-to-toe in all but the veil — was just across the yard at the foot of the stairway, watering a vine which twisted up through the stone. Its leaves spread over an open door.

Eve nodded hello, the woman beckoned her over. She spoke only Moghrebi but quickly established, with much animation, that she was Madame Djerid, that her black attire was because of her husband who now, Allah be praised, was at rest; that her own food was ready and Eve was to join her.

Inside, on a charcoal *mijmah*, water was already boiling. She was handed mint tea in a tiny handleless cup, then offered dates and something like cold semolina, but stickier, sweeter. Eve found the tea just as sickly, but forced back the traditional third glass before feeling able to leave.

At the grungy *daïra* she registered her arrival and enquired as to Larcum's whereabouts. The official checking her passport referred to him as 'Monsieur Ari'. Gave directions to a house called Riad-ez-Hamid, only two streets away.

She rapped twice on a door in the wall and waited for almost a minute before a striking Arab — sinewy and compact, thirtyish, with sharp narrow eyes like a fox — opened the door just enough to reveal his face and a glimpse of sizeable patio behind. Fig tree, brilliant mimosa spread across the far wall.

'Sidi he busy now,' the man informed her. 'He expects you?'

'Not exactly . . .'

Lifting the sleeve of his *djellaba* the man glanced at a flashy gold watch. Then made to close the gate on her.

'Wait!' she said. 'Please. If you'll just give him this.'

Reaching into her carry-all Eve handed the man the folder she'd prepared. Early on she had decided that writing to Larcum in advance would be a mistake. It was well known that since coming to Mohkran he'd granted no interviews, and isolation made it easy to say no from a distance. Her best chance, she'd figured, was simply to present herself; bank on him being intrigued, admiring her resolve and credentials — in particular the photo she'd clipped in the folder.

The factotum narrowed his eyes still further, examining both her and the file with suspicion. Then with the faintest of nods he reached out and took it.

'*Attendez*,' he declared.

It seemed interminable, the time she was left there. The heat was already intense. A bent old man trudged by, leading a mule on a limp length of rope. Baskets piled with lemons knocked at the animal's flanks. By now she had seated herself in the shade of the gateway opposite Larcum's. She made a curious spectacle, she supposed—spiky black hair, Ray Bans, fanning herself with her tattered cabaña straw hat. Her time in Algiers had taught her that when they looked at you it was sometimes curiosity but most often contempt. Sitting there she found her thoughts drifting to the time she dropped out of the Juilliard, began running errands for the guys at *Probe*. Nearly eight years ago. Eight years, preparing for this. And always the chance he might die before she was ready. But somehow she'd known that he wouldn't—maybe *couldn't*—before it was done. And done right.

Presently—it had been at least twenty minutes—the door reopened and the Arab signaled to her to enter. It seemed to Eve that he did so reluctantly, even now. Silently he preceded her across the patio, through a Moorish arch and up to an open-sided second-floor balcony like a cloister. They came to a curtain: the man drew it back, stood to one side.

Before her as she entered was a long spacious room. Like her own it was low-ceilinged, sparsely furnished. But here everything was polished, swept: she could tell this at once, despite the dimness. Both windows in the wall to her left were shuttered. What little light there was appeared at first to have only one source: at the far end of the room a small fire was burning, crackling bluely in a

square solid hearth. It was hard to believe her own eyes:
110° in the shade, and he wanted a *fire*? Notwithstanding
its size the room felt airless, almost hermetically sealed.

'Ah, Miss West. Come and make yourself comfortable.'

She started a little, looked again, still seeing no one.
Then something moved to the right of the chimney-
breast: a shadow that deepened, climbed to the ceiling
and sped across it to meet her as a bulky figure rose with
a grunt of difficulty from the corner. He wore a long,
pale, tent-like *gandoura* and for a moment — unprepared at
finding him in native dress — she assumed it to be someone
else, another guest perhaps. His softly pitched voice made
this equally plausible: the intonation was strange, faintly
uncertain, as though English was now foreign to him.

'An unexpected pleasure, this. You've caught us by
surprise, I'm afraid . . . visitors are few these days.'

She came forward. Noticed, where he had been, a
lamp on the floor. From under its shade it cast a small
yellow circle on a scatter of cushions, one propped against
the wall as a back-rest.

For how long had she imagined this moment — the
anger, the bitterness she'd feel — finally crossing a room to
meet him? The truth was, now it was actually happening,
she simply felt numb.

She'd expected him older, more lined, but he was still
recognisably the Harry Larcum of her outdated press pic-
tures. Taller than she'd imagined; bigger all round. The
thick crinkly hair, very white, showed no sign of receding on his sun-darkened head. She noted, too, the fleshy,
rather prominent ears which in photos always made her
recoil. There may have been a slight limp as he moved to
greet her, but though she'd steeled herself against sympathy — the chance of finding him infirm or decrepit — he

looked in remarkable shape for a man over seventy. Fit, she decided, for all she could throw at him.

'Sit down, sit down.' He smiled and waved an arm vaguely. More cushions lay about on small Berber rugs. She was relieved he didn't expect to shake hands or, worse still, kiss her.

Removing her shoulder-bag she settled herself next to a cedarwood chest which sat squarely back from the fire. Several scuffed books lay upon it haphazardly. From what she could see they weren't Larcum titles. Indeed, apart from the modest glass-fronted bookcase (dwarfed by a wall ten metres long and otherwise blank) evidence of his profession was as sparse as the room.

'You'll take tea with me?'

The last thing she wanted was more cloying mint. 'Thanks' she said, all the same. 'That'd be nice.'

The warmth of the welcome, in every sense, had rather unsettled her. Larcum clapped his hands, called out 'Mahmoud!' in the same light tone. The man who'd admitted her reappeared, soundlessly.

'*Joosh atay. Bisora*,' said Larcum and the Arab nodded curtly. As he left she saw him glance at her sidelong: the same narrow-eyed look of mistrust.

'Oh, and fetch some more wood,' Larcum called after him. 'The fire's burning low.'

'Sorry about earlier,' he went on. Warming his hands behind him he stood right in front of the flames. 'I breakfast with the *caïd* on Wednesdays. Long-standing arrangement. He comes here, I go to him. Hence the . . .'

He flicked his *gandoura*. OK, formality might account for it partly, but she still knew a poser when she saw one.

He used to rock back and forth on his toes . . . hold court on the platform, pleased as you like . . .

It was Mo's voice — coming back to her, clear as a

bell, as she watched him. And now here he was, rocking gently in his worn babouche slippers. Up and down, almost imperceptibly.

. . . soft baby-blue eyes and come-to-me voice. Like some smarmy preacher set on seduction . . .

'Strordin'ry fellow, *caïd* bin Hami,' Larcum was saying. 'Read more Dickens than I have! Give him half a chance, he'll recite you the Getysburg Address!' Turning away he moved back to his nook of cushions.

Loved himself?— You'd better believe it. Then again, he was some looking guy . . . guess he thought he had reason.

And he had presence, that Eve conceded. As for charm, it went without saying.

'Well, you've come a long way,' he said. 'I'm flattered.'

But each time he smiled at her she felt her skin tighten. She might not be the foxiest thing on two legs, but she was young and a woman, and the glint in his eyes confirmed all Mo had said. She began to understand—given the glamour surrounding his early success—how she'd succumbed.

The servant reappeared with an armful of logs, some more charcoal.

'Damned circulation,' the old man shivered, rubbing his arm. 'My whole system's on strike.' Mahmoud vanished again having poked at the grate. The fire flared, started to crackle.

'I didn't realise, I'm sorry.'

'*Pff*! Nothing really. This hand's the worst part.' He made a fist; spread his fingers and waggled them. 'Mind of its own. Some morning's I have to warm up, that's all . . . bask like a lizard a while!' He chuckled. 'Pen goes a bit haywire sometimes.'

'You've seen someone? A doctor, I mean.'

'My dear, your sympathy's touching,' he inclined his

head, 'but let's not overplay it. That's accent's not native East Coast? Or are my ears going too?'

She dredged up a smile. 'I'm impressed.' Well, wasn't she meant to be? No point not indulging the bastard, at least for now. 'Two generation's back. My mother's side . . .'

'No, don't tell me.' He held up a hand. 'Professional pride. Silly, but . . . Give me a moment, I'll pin you down.'

She looked for signs of innuendo but he seemed unaware, continuing blithely: 'Your parents still alive then?'

'One is.'

It was time she got back on track. She was supposed to be asking the questions.

'Mo — my mother — she died when I was fifteen. Cancer, they said.' And at once Eve cursed herself. She hadn't meant to mention Mo, not this early at least. Still, he'd known her as Jo, of course, or Jo-Anne. Mo was her own private name, daughter to mother.

'"They said?"' Larcum echoed. 'You sound doubtful.'

'Oh, it was cancer, OK. But what does that prove?' She knew she should kill the subject, and fast. But rising anger inspired her. 'It's what *causes* the cancer, right? And who bothers with that? You know that box on the death certificate? It's too small for the truth, so they write "Carcinoma".'

She stopped short, aware suddenly of how he was studying her. Dumb bitch, she upbraided herself. Get a hold.

'Please. Forget it.'

To hide her discomposure she reached across and fumbled about in her bag. Checked that the small red recording light still glowed on the recorder. Then extracted the clipboard with her few token questions and replaced the bag, as though casually, with its open end facing him.

'You're still writing then?'

Larcum hesitated, she thought, then gave the same little chuckle. 'That surprises you?'

'In a way. You've published nothing for nearly ten years.'

'Yes, that's true.' He nodded to himself and the heavy brows lifted a fraction, as though this had only now struck him. 'Too busy, I suppose. Busy writing. Reflecting. There comes a time, you know.' The firelight gleamed in his eyes as he looked past her. 'Sometimes I think I *see* death. See it walking towards me.'

He reached down, picked up a pack of cigarettes, a black holder. They looked like cheroots. He offered her one and she declined.

'Why *should* I publish?' he went on, exhaling a fine grey smoke. 'To satisfy others? *Their* curiosity? I did that for as long as I had to. Now I write for myself . . . what I want. Freedom and pleasure — that's what I have here.'

'And responsibility?' she asked.

He regarded her quizzically. 'Responsibility? That's a strange question. To who? To what? Or do you mean,' he smiled, 'my extraordinary talent?'

'I was thinking more of your readers.'

'My dear girl. I learnt soon enough about the fickleness of readers. Their taste is mostly appalling, so why should it detain me?' He took another drag. 'If any Larcum readers remain — which judging by my last royalty statement is *highly* questionable — then they're fools . . . gullible, unthinking fools.'

Wow, that was perfect. She could see the headline already: MY READERS ARE FOOLS.

At which point Mahmoud arrived with the tea.

❧

'You're at Lalla Djerid's?'

She nodded.

'Hardly the Algonquin, I'm afraid.' The glass steamed as he drank.

'It's OK.'

She sipped a little as well—from her glass in a silver-filagree holder. The sweet aroma alone made her nauseous. She set the glass on the chest.

'You don't take many notes,' Larcum observed, nodding at the board on her knee.

'No,' she replied evenly, though she felt her pulse skip. 'I remember what's important. And the job's about making you comfortable.'

'Well, thank's for that. Least you're not recording. Never could stand it—felt like my soul was . . .'

'Sorry,' she cut in, as if it had just occurred to her. 'But while I remember . . . Those ruins near here . . . the old palace . . .' She improvised wildly, anything to move him on. 'Worth seeing, d'you think?'

'I assume you mean Ksar Zulten. More fortress than palace, in fact. Twelfth century . . .'

Larcum seemed unfazed by her change of direction.

'Yes, an interesting place,' he was saying. 'Has atmosphere, certainly. You'd need a guide, of course. And transport.'

'I'm sorry?'

'To get there. It's a fair way . . . pretty inaccessible.' He paused. 'If you want I'll make some enquiries.

'Sure. . . yeah. That'd be good.'

Well, she could back out if need be. At least the diversion had served its purpose.

'So, this article,' he resumed. 'What ground are you hoping to cover? I'm not clear exactly.'

Old ground, she thought. Tainted ground. But gave him her sweetest smile. 'Be nice to know how you came to be here. Why the retreat? That kinda thing. Nothing controversial.'

'Hah! Now I *know* I'm in trouble! Who'll give a damn *unless* it's controversial?' He drank some more, eyes twinkling over his glass. 'Don't worry, my dear. Just an old man having his fun. Go ahead, I'll tell you what I can.'

'Just the truth,' she said. 'That's all I'm after.'

'The truth? Well, that's asking a lot. Invention's simpler, you know. More fun. Sells better too.'

'You agree it was facile then? The success?'

'Facile,' he repeated again, weighing the word. 'About the sum of it, yes. Best-sellers to others, sell-outs to me.' He smiled wryly. 'That's a bit hard perhaps. I had *facility*, no doubting that. *The Dark Sea . . . Oliver's Secret*—those first ones had something. Don't you think?'

He sighed, ground out the cheroot.

'I looked at them not long ago. Not bad for a jumped-up kid, an ironmonger's lad. I was surprised. But that was the best of me. After that all the nonsense began . . . the publicity. What's worse, I *believed* it.' She watched him raise a hand, rub his eyes. 'No, can't say much for that person, not now.'

He looked up at her and she thought: You're old news, Larcum. Finished.

'You see, I did understand in the end. That was when I knew I had to get away.'

She felt a new and strange atmosphere in the room; as though something was suspended, invisibly, between them. A flutter of sparks flew away up the chimney.

'There was a globe that sat in the window next to my

desk. Ibiza, this was. I used to spin it while I was thinking. For hours sometimes. Here they have beads, of course.'

He smiled to himself, leaned back in the cushions. His face was yellow as parchment in the lamplight, his eyes blocks of shadow.

'The view of the bay was breathtaking, I never tired of it . . . the white waves, the rocks. Anyway, this particular time was different. I kept thinking of Russian roulette. You know — spinning and spinning the chamber. I'd made a pact with myself, I suppose. Move on or . . .'

He paused again.

'My finger kept landing at sea though. Time and again, like some terrible joke. As if there was no choice . . . as if I was drowning anyway. This make any sense?'

It sounded like bull, but she nodded.

'And once it came down on land — El Oued, the Sahara — it seemed just as hopeless.' He turned to her. 'You'll stop me if this is no use.'

See, she thought, *just another story*. She was sure he could summon up countless alternatives.

'I flew down the same week, felt compelled to, simply to look. But as soon as I got out here — the desert — I knew. It wasn't madness, it was sanity. This was the *only* place to come to. I flew home, sold the house . . . everything bar a few books. Three months later I was back in Mohkran. For good.'

He picked up his glass, raised it half-way to his lips before seeing it was empty. 'I came in in full Arab dress. Oh, far grander than this,' he chuckled, fingering the *gan-doura*. 'The *caïd* had lent me his favourite camel . . . and two more for the books! You think the Mohkranis stare at you? You should've seen them that day!'

His laugh dissolved into a dry, hacking cough. She took the glass from his outstretched hand and refilled it.

'So you set up as some kind of hermit?'

'Well, it's rather more basic than Ibiza,' he nodded, looking about him as he passed a handkerchief over his mouth. 'But I wouldn't say hermit-like, no.'

'Not the hair-shirt then?

'Now, now. Let's not get religious.'

'Retreating . . . atoning for the past, I was thinking. 'Selling out.' *Your* words.'

'My dear, we all have regrets. That's life. Escape, I'm speaking of. Not self-flagellation. Why should I have cause to atone?'

'You tell me.'

His eyes narrowed. She felt them scanning her face closely, disconcertingly. Still, she felt certain her appearance provided no clue. With her height and dark hair she looked nothing like Mo. Nor him, for that matter. No, he didn't know she existed. Wouldn't care if he had.

Larcum pushed himself up with a groan. Back in front of the fire, he looked down at her.

'I trust you're not like the others, Miss West,' he said with a new and discernible coolness. Almost like a warning. 'Don't take me for a fool.'

'Others?'

'Oh, certain colleagues of yours. Or should I say "rivals". None came to cause trouble, naturally. None came 'to pry'.' He forced an empty smile. 'I've no wish to be unchivalrous, my dear . . . but do remember you're my guest here. Hmm?'

She caught another whiff of his arrogance, condescension. Talking down to her as, doubtless, he had to Mo . . . every audience and reader he'd addressed. His adoring public, the ones he secretly despised. Lecturing her, she thought with irony, like his own goddam daughter.

'Good, I'm glad we understand one another. Because

I enjoy a woman's company, I admit. It's something I miss here.'

Striving to conceal her anger, certain of her rising colour, Eve inclined her head as if in acknowledgement. It occurred to her that maybe some vestigial intuition *did* still connect them; something she'd never considered.

'I've never denied it. Women inspire me — always have. It's as simple as that. We're a cantankerous, self-absorbed lot, us *"artistes"*. Shut ourselves away, pretend we can cope without others, but we all need *someone* . . . sometimes.' He shrugged. 'Certain people only work out of pain. I needed happiness. Women made me happy.'

'And you them?'

He lit another cheroot.

'One rarely acts as honourably as one could. *C'est la vie encore*. I wouldn't wish living with a writer on anyone . . . then again, I was lucky. Very. Most claimed they understood.'

She looked away in distaste as smoke blew from his nostrils. She had a strong sense of Mo's presence, here in the room with her.

'So,' he concluded. 'What are you thinking?'

Inwardly she took a deep breath. 'I'm thinking "thinking's bad for me sometimes". I guess I'm more . . .' Her fist had clenched tight. She pressed it to her abdomen. 'It comes from in here.'

'Ah,' Larcum nodded. 'Visceral, you mean. That too can be highly creative, of course.'

He looked at his watch. 'Well, my dear, we can always continue tomorrow, but now I'm afraid . . .'

'Oh, sure.' She reached for her bag.

'Has it been helpful? I hope so.'

'Oh yes. Very. So when shall we . . .'

She'd risen, a little dizzily, and all at once was conscious of a rushing sound that seemed to emanate within her own ears. Grasping the clipboard she looked down just as the first spatters of red struck it, like ink-blots.

'Dammit!' she exclaimed and threw back her head. Tried to sit down again, feeling for the cushions behind her. 'I'm sorry . . . do you have a tissue? '

'Mahmoud!' Larcum called. Again the rat-tat of hands.

'Here, my dear . . .' He came across. She felt him take her arm, the board eased from her hand and a handkerchief replace it. She held it to her nose.

'Not to worry. Just rest for a moment . . . over here.'

He led her to where she could prop herself against the wall between the two fastened shutters. When she swallowed the taste of blood almost made her throw up.

'I'm sorry,' she said, despite herself.

'Don't be silly. I used to suffer badly. It's the dryness . . . takes a while to get used to.'

Mahmoud arrived, was despatched, and seconds later returned with a small rock of ice. Pressed to the back of her neck, then her forehead, it felt wonderful. Well before the ice had dissolved the bleeding had stopped.

'The fire can't have helped,' Larcum said. 'Thoughtless of me.'

She got up gingerly. Mahmoud remained, hovering near the curtain — still, it appeared, unconvinced. As if she had staged the whole thing.

'Tomorrow we can sit in the garden', Larcum continued, hobbling the length of the room with her. 'If you'd care to come a little earlier.'

She glanced at him. 'I'm still welcome then?'

'My dear Miss West, you take yourself too seriously.' She hadn't succeeded in wiping the smile from his face.

'The light's beautiful now,' she remarked downstairs

as they stepped into the courtyard. 'I'd like to get a photo
. . . would you mind?'

'*Pas de tout.* Where do you want me? Over here by my
fruit trees?'

With one of the gallery arches framing him perfectly
he struck a studious pose—favouring the left profile. He
hadn't forgotten how.

'OK, just hold it.' Quickly she took three or four shots,
laying it on thick as she did so. 'This is one big break for
me, you know that? Really, I'm grateful.'

She steeled herself as he approached, unable to deflect
his peck at each cheek.

'Tomorrow then. Mahmoud will see you out.'

Like a grotesque genie the Arab materialised from
nowhere and preceded her to the gate. Eve was beginning
to sense he was too sure of himself to be merely a servant.
Servants might be protective, sure, but it struck her now
that the warnings she'd read in his eyes were more those
reserved for a rival in love. Who knows where Larcum's
eye roved, she thought with disgust. There was no taboo
here, of course.

Another angle she could work on.

It was after midday, but the narrow tunnel-like alleys
were still deep in shadow. Since the place was too small
to get lost in, she decided to wander a little. Her main
concern, apart from keeping out of the sun and finding a
drink, was avoiding the kids. Having failed to reach her
last night something told her they'd be waiting in ambush
somewhere. Little savages, she smiled to herself, rounding
another corner warily. She could already picture the bone
bracelets, necklaces, all the other crap they'd shove in her
face and expect her to buy. Some, no doubt, were simply
beggars or thieves. Well, they needn't expect to panhandle

off *her*. New York hardened anyone. You just had to be clear from the start.

The mud-red walls were windowless and steep: she could have stretched out and touched both sides at once. Now and then a hot flurry of wind came chasing after her, scouring her bare arms with particles of sand. Still she had encountered no one. Somewhere she heard a shutter or door creak open; then, at some distance, a muffled hubbub of sound—more a hum than distinguishable voices. The market, she supposed, recalling that Larcum had told her this was the last before Id el Adha, the final chance to purchase one's sacrifice. Apparently some Chaamba had driven in a new flock this morning. Larcum's joke—'*Everyone* makes a killing this time of year!'—she'd found almost funny.

'The selling goes on all day,' he'd said. 'You really should see it.'

She'd go, but later. Right now, their meeting still fresh in her mind, she needed to reassess certain things, sketch in more detail. Check the tape. She'd expected to feel high at this moment, elated. But for some reason she couldn't determine she felt gripped by unease.

Stirred by her passing, a cloud of flies buzzed drowsily from a pile of camel droppings; settled again within seconds.

Back in her room she rewound the tape. With the volume full-on she could pick up Larcum quite clearly. She breathed a sigh of relief. Inserting a new blank cassette, she dropped the used one into her case. Fast as she could she scribbled down in shorthand everything she recalled of the room and the house . . . the reptilian Mahmoud, the heat and dark of the room, Harry Larcum's appearance, mannerisms. When she could think of no more she sat back with the pad on her knee and tried again with the letter to Ed.

But it was hopeless: she just couldn't concentrate. She crumpled a third sheet of paper and tossed it aside. It fell in the corner where she'd thrown yesterday's clothes, ready for washing. May as well take care of them now, she thought; then the market.

Down in the sluice-yard were a couple of buckets and a well; two rudimentary, shoulder-high screens. Also some soapy-wet scrubbing boards. As she came down the steps she heard a sloshing of water, saw a figure crouched over the boards, a yellow sarong-like towel round his waist.

'Hi,' she said brightly, taking him in.

He paused and looked up. Very blonde, Nordic, lean and tanned. Wet hair straggly and long. The guy's looks were just fine but his presence bugged her at once. Another visitor in Mohkran spoilt her theory — that nobody but her had reason to be here.

She took the other board and got on with her chore beside him. Now and then, in a polite kind of way, she tried quizzing him as they scrubbed; but her mind was edgy. Anyhow, mostly he just smiled to himself, not saying much. All she really got was his name — Mati — that he was 24 (though he looked barely 20) and came from a place near Helsinki. Still, she was happy just looking.

He'd been here only two days himself. It pleased her to learn that he'd come by sheer chance — 'I like the name — Mohk-raaaan. It makes a good sound, yes?' — and finally began to lower her guard. Best of all, he'd not even heard of Larcum.

'You serious?' she laughed. It made him pretty unique.

'I do not read books. Time is for doing, yes?'

He spoke so carefully, so *seriously*, she was tempted to laugh. But thinking about it, maybe he had something. She liked crazy ideas. Yeah, maybe only those who couldn't face life had to read of it. Anyhow, when she decided that Huck was a good name for Mati ('Huck *Finn*, right?') the joke was lost on the guy since he didn't know of Twain either. She shook her head, grinning. He had to be kidding her.

He said the light stuff would dry where it was, dripping over a wire. She followed his lead and carried her wrung-out towel upstairs to lay on the sill. He took a look at her room and she his. It was identical except for the absence of a hatch to the roof. They went up on her's for a minute, but the heat was like an iron, the light too intense. The sky was bleached white. They were frying.

'Where'd you find a drink around here?' she asked him. A *real* drink, she meant, though she knew the odds were long. To her amazement Mati said 'Sure, Néma's has beer, anisette . . . many things.'

'Not an iced Tom Collins, I bet!'

She suggested they go along now. Mati said he'd show her the place, but couldn't stay himself.

'Néma asks me to his garden in the *palmeraie*,' he said as they descended to the room. 'He has a small house there. We drink tea, he says, smoke a little . . . Néma he plays the *qsbah* also.'

'How nice,' she replied, slightly irked to be told of all this yet excluded. Specially from the smoking. She'd tried some *kif* in Algiers, still had some over.

'You are liking to come?' Mati added, as if telepathic. 'Maybe I . . .'

'Thanks,' she said, 'but I've things to do too.' Why did she care what he did? Was he worth spending time with anyhow? Hell, if he laid back much further he'd be plain horizontal! It crossed her mind to let him know her true reason for coming to Mohkran — if only to get some reaction — but on reflection decided that would be crazy. Later, maybe, once everything was safely on record.

They were at the door when a sudden commotion below drew them back to the window. Another high-pitched shriek, a dull thud. Down in Mme Djerid's patio, the *propriétaire* stood with her back to them, swinging something, hard and repeatedly, into one of the walls. Eve assumed at first it was washing but, once the woman was still, saw she was holding a small pale snake. Its pulverised head dripped redly on the sand. Turning, Mme D caught sight of them and beamed. Called something out, showing her catch proudly. Then, still holding it at arm's length, she disappeared inside.

As they went down the street (it turned out Néma was the Sundanese guy who had seen her arrive, the burrow in the wall his so-called café), Eve realised the incident had affected her markedly. She kept seeing the snake's pulpy head, as if in close-up. She tried explaining this to Mati but all he could say was: 'Yah, don't go bare feet. Nowhere, OK?' — in his spacey monotone as they ducked into the gloom.

'There are scorpions also. You look careful in your shoe in the morning, yah?'

'Gee, thanks,' Eve muttered.

She pushed up her shades but even then took a moment to adjust. Dingy and flyblown, a few plank tables scattered about. At one of them four grizzled men playing dice paused to glower as they entered. Once she'd said hi to Néma and he and Mati had set off for the *palmeraie* (leaving Néma's young son in charge) she stayed just long enough to throw back a *biére Algérienne* — even flattish and warm it revived her — before leaving herself. Mati had said Néma's wife was preparing tajine for the customers tonight; told Eve he'd meet her there around seven. And she'd replied 'Maybe.'

She found the *souq* wedged between the water-course and the edge of the village in a long single strip. Well before she reached there the bleating served as her guide. Rudimentary stalls backed onto the bank of the *seguia*, stretching between its two simple causeways. Overhead canopies of palm fronds and rushes, absent in patches, gave a dappled lattice-like shade; yet even this fragile canopy seemed to lock in below it the heat, the noise, the dizzying amalgam of perfume and bestial odour.

It was a shock, too, to find so many people. She realised that hitherto she'd seen no more than a handful at any one time — in the café, outside the mosque before prayer, the urchin mob — so that her mind had begun to accept such numbers as the limit of Mohkran's population. Now, bumped and jostled, she had no option but to let the tide take her — hemmed between hooded figures, hamstrung animals, pyramids of spice — a throng unlike any she was familiar with. And yet, in the strangest way, she felt safe.

Her eye was caught by a sudden, dazzling reflection. Ahead she made out a wizened old Arab in a thick brown *burnous*, hunched on a mat in the dirt. Before him all manner of knives were spread out on pieces of sacking. Behind and above him, still more hung from makeshift hooks in the wall. It was these which stirred gently like sinister wind-chimes, flashing as light caught them. She saw butcher-sized cleavers, serpentine daggers with elaborate hilts, plain kitchen knives.

A knot of potential customers lingered in front of the display. She edged in beside a veiled, almost square woman, busy inspecting a particular blade. Eve watched as she drew it in and out of its sheath of pale goathide, a small pointed boning knife with a hasp of dark, knotted wood—olive, she thought. It was beautiful in its way. The woman called out a price through her muslin-like *sibniya*: the old man spat back his response without moving. The fat matron threw up her hands, tossed the knife down histrionically and pushed back into the crowd.

Bending forward, Eve took up the knife herself. The sheath was warm and soft, the twists of the grip moulded at once to her hand.

'*Kem dinar?*' she found herself asking.

The same grunted answer. Seventy dinars. Ten dollars, near enough. To him, as she knew, a ridiculous sum.

Not to bargain was a sign of weakness, she knew that. She could sense those around her, the old stall-keeper himself, sneering contemptuously as she handed over the money. But so what? She had no memento of the desert bar this. And to her it was cheap.

She was approaching the cut that led down to the Pension Djerid when she noticed a figure emerge from it hurriedly and, without breaking stride, sweep off in the opposite direction. Even from behind she recognised Larcum's factotum immediately. The same feline walk, the black-striped *djellaba*: there was no mistaking him. She watched the turning he took up ahead, just to make doubly sure. Yes, returning to the Riad-ez-Hamid like a good errand boy. What the hell did *he* want?

She walked quickly down the alley and let herself through the outer door with the key Madame Djerid had given her. Took the steps to the gallery two at a time. She had no doubt, suddenly, that Mahmoud had been here, in her room. A hot wave broke over her as she thought of the tape. Had Larcum sent him? Had he taken it on himself?

Inside she found an envelope just under the door. She

picked it up. It seemed to her there was a strange smell in the room, a faint mustiness, even though the shutter lay open. She went at once to the case, lifted it onto the bed. The recorder was there and, more important, the tape. Nothing *appeared* to be missing—but then the contents had been a mess in the first place. It was impossible to say they hadn't been searched.

Her skull was thudding like crazy. She sat down and undid the envelope. It was a note from Larcum:

Regret best guide to Ksar Zulten is absent (haj to Mecca) but idea occurs. Allow me to show you. Haven't been for years but know its history. Also the route—not unimportant! Forgive presumption: have spoken with Caïd bin Hami. He's cleared us to go & will lend his jeep. (Do you drive? I thought we might share that between us).

We can chat as easily on the way. Trust you approve. If OK, be at the caïd's, 7am tomorrow. If no-go, send word before 9 tonight.

Regards, H.L.

'Shit,' she muttered. Now what?

She was here to see Larcum, sure, but not to trek round the desert with him, not in this heat. *Specially* not to gawp at some heap of tumbledown rocks! Trouble was, she saw now she'd have to fall in with it, even act grateful.

She swallowed more pills for her head and lay down. It dawned on her that Larcum might be using the ruins for a plan of his own. Maybe he intended to confront her tomorrow, turn the tables in some way. Well, it really didn't matter now. She smiled faintly, picturing his face when she told him. That his past was no secret to her would soon be public knowledge.

For pity's sake, child . . . I'm an old man now . . .

She could hear his cracked voice. *Pity*? Was he serious? What pity had *he* shown? 'Old man?' Not too old for some things, right? Ready for any young girl who just happened by . . .

She sat up sharply. Jeez, you dumb bitch! Was *that* why he wanted to get her there—away from Mohkran, alone?

A shiver of revulsion passed through her, tinged now with fear. Surely, not even *he* would try that.

She caught sight of the knife on the table. From here on, she thought, it stayed with her, regardless.

'So,' Mati asked slowly, 'he is what kind of man, this writer?'

They sat alone in the back room at Néma's.

'Know what I think?' Eve replied. 'The guy stinks.' She said it as much to convince herself as to answer his question. Once again she examined Mati over their plates. His skin glistened in the light of the lamp. What she *really* wanted to tell him was everything, the whole story. Uncertain how to handle tomorrow, she could've used another head. He and Néma, however, had clearly been smoking the whole afternoon: now the owner sat slumped behind the counter twiddling the radio between stations and Mati looked in much the same stupor, his lazy eyes even dreamier than before. There was no point then. Anyway, where would she start? With Larcum walking out on Mo? With Jack West, the surgeon who'd delivered her, whose name she had taken? Her dreams of the stage? Or Mo falling sick, how that had changed everything; how only in the hospital she'd learnt the truth about her real father?

Instead she just sighed and said: 'I need another drink.'

She looked away through the arch to the inner room. Two steps down she could see part of the counter, the hard blue flame of the primus. Abdeslem, Néma's small son, hurried back and forth, ferrying tea.

'You think people care about him? So many people?' Mati said languidly, not taking his eyes from his food. He'd planted his elbows square on the table now, his orange-greased fingers hanging over the plate. The tajine, in fact, didn't strike her as anything special; but maybe they were saving the tenderest lambs for the Feast. After tomorrow the slaughter would start.

She wanted to say she'd lost sight of the person she'd been before learning of Larcum. But nobody, even sober, could possibly understand. That this trip was more than just getting even. That it went to the core of her being. For so long her very existence seemed solely confirmed by her pain. *I hurt, therefore I am.* Without the anger and bitterness which stabbed her inside she sometimes feared she would prove to be nothing. Not human, anyway. A formless, unfeeling thing.

'You do not eat?' Mati, frowning with the effort of speaking, watched her push her plate aside.

'I've no appetite. It's the heat maybe.'

'This is why you are thin like the sparrow?' He smiled. 'No, I am liking the sparrows. But even they eat a little.'

'In Algiers,' she said, 'I found this place in the Kasbah. It was OK, I guess, but you know what? All the locals had burgers and fries. I'm serious. You just wouldn't believe.'

Mati shrugged. 'We all like the taste of each other.'

He had another beer, then a *lagmi*—the local firewater. Strangely the more he drank the soberer he appeared to become. Maybe alcohol negated the dope. In any case, his speech wasn't slurred now. The other room was gradually quietening. They could hear the radio more clearly—no longer the swooping Islamic vocalist, but a gutteral voice talking Arabic, fast and intently.

'Eve? Do you listen?'

'Huh? Why, what is it?'

'Is news from Algiers. There is trouble, big trouble.' Mati cocked his head, listening. It was clear he'd picked up the language quickly during his months in the Mogreb. 'Early tonight. Many windows broken . . . They turn over cars—big Nazarene cars, Mercedes . . . make them burn.'

'Jeez,' she murmured. May be she *hadn't* imagined the pressure then. And now it had blown.

'What's it all about?'

'Prices,' he shrugged. 'Food. They cannot buy bread now'.

Her thoughts raced. The story was falling into place, backdrop and detail. Riots . . . Sacrifice . . . LARCUM SCORNS READERS . . . TRIES TO MAKE HIS OWN DAUGHTER . . . The whole world would be buying. All at once her doubts fled. She finished the anisette the boy had brought her.

'Time we were going, huh?'

They stood up. Mati towered over her, his shadow dancing behind him. Just then, from a hiccup of static, a pulsing dance-beat rhythm leapt at them out of the night. She started with shock, saw Mati grimace. Néma stepped up through the archway, grinning broadly. He held the radio on one shoulder, close to his ear; his white teeth made him seem blacker than ever. A thin, child-woman's voice was singing. Words dimly familiar:

Borderline . . . feels like I'm going to lose m'mind
You just keep on pushin' my love . . . over the borderline . . .
Jesus, it was Madonna.

'G-oo-d, *n'est pas*?' Néma swayed lazily in a semblance of dance. '*Éro-tique, ca femme*?'

Mati still had his eyes screwed up. Eve let her head loll back as she laughed. It was all too much. She'd never be able to explain: not to Larcum, not to Mati, not to anyone. It was crazy. The whole damned thing.

'Come on, let's get out of here,' she said.

They went back to her room and smoked the last of her kif from Algiers. As her head filled she drew farther and farther away from herself. Above through the trap the stars throbbed and pulsed.

'You strange lady, Eve.' His hand touched her cheek. 'You don't tell what you want.'

'Maybe I don't know yet.' She placed her hand on his, then pulled him to her. 'Come on, Huck, make me forget.'

Here was the fjord she could drown in. She swam mindlessly, sinking deeper. Once she thought she heard someone calling—saw a veiled women somewhere below them. When finally he took hold of her, held her down, she cried out to the night, past all resistance, her back turned not only on him but the past.

Later she dreamed she was walking the shore on Long Island, a child again. Jack and Mo had driven her out there to see Grammie Eth. She walked in her party dress, holding her shoes. Only now she was able to watch herself, as if from outside. See her bare foot approaching the jellyfish washed up on the sand. Anticipate the sharp stab of pain, the aching that ebbed and returned like the tide. Her tears wouldn't cease, and when nobody came she waded out in the surf to seek comfort. It rose and fell about her, picked her up and caressed her till the shore disappeared. She was naked now, floating, exposed to the white sun above. Then she saw the pale gelatinous shoal on the swell. Lay and watched it wash closer . . . closer . . . and finally against her.

Rising, she pushed open the shutter. Behind the big dune

lay the white thread of dawn. Her mind was quite clear now. She knew what had to be done and set about each task mechanically.

Ed, honey, she wrote,

I'm sorry, but we'd just never make it. I hoped you'd see it for yourself—and maybe you have now—but holding out on you was one big mistake.

I know what you're thinking, but there's nobody else. Going away's let me see what I couldn't close-up, that's all. You mustn't expect to see me again, at least for some time.

Forgive me.

When she'd finished she stood her small mirror on the sill and smoothed some cream on her face. Her grey-green eyes stared back, unblinking. From her purse she took out the photo of Mo she'd brought with her, placing it with care in her pocket. Then she dressed, drank some water and zipped up the bags.

Downstairs she left them with Mme Djerid, made clear she'd be back.

The warm wind had sprung up again. It came and went in sharp, irregular gusts, sucking up spirals of sand.

Outside the *caïd*'s she saw several silhouettes bent round the jeep. Its hood was up, a beam of torchlight playing behind it.

'*Ah, voilà. Elle arrive,*' came a voice she recognised. Larcum emerged from the huddle, came toward her. He was dressed differently today: no *gandoura*, no slippers. Instead an open-necked shirt, light cotton trousers, beach shoes.

'Am I late then?'

'No-no. Just some last-minute checks. Want to throw that inside?' He nodded at her carry-all.

'It's OK. I'll keep it with me.'

She looked about for Mahmoud and noticed him

hovering in the background. His master's shadow. It struck
Eve that maybe he was trying to tag along. Strangely, part
of her now hoped he would.

She climbed in the front. Behind her were spare cans
of gasoline, water; also an ice-box, she noticed. At length
Larcum got in.

'All set then? Right, we're off.'

Within minutes they were progressing at speed down
the bitumen highway. A sign zipped by: *Frontière Tunisi-
enne* — *40 kms*. Arm on the sill in the almost-cool slipstream, she watched the first faint pinks backlighting the
ridges. She said she'd take over the wheel while the road
was good — she'd rather drive here that on sand — but
Larcum claimed to be happy. For some while after this
neither spoke. The jeep whistled on.

'How far did you say?' she asked presently.

'An hour, perhaps less. Depends what we find when
we turn off again. This wind might've covered the tracks.'

The sun broke over the dunes like a nuclear flash. She
dug out her glasses as Larcum headed left into the sand. A
board, its lettering faded, was nailed to lopsided post: *À
Ksar Zul . . . Interdit Sauf Permi . . .*

The piste was rutted now — shallow parallel depres-
sions. Now and then a red buoy-like marker loomed up.

'Not long now,' he said.

When the edifice finally came into view, stark against
the sky, it reminded her of a vast yellowish termite mound
from which the upper half had crumbled and fallen. The
jagged parapets gaped openly at the sky. A lone arch, now
gateless, stood dark at the centre, the lopsided remnant
of a honeycombed tower at one corner. A stunted acacia
thorn stood some distance away, its boughs gently astir.
Before Larcum had brought the jeep to a standstill she had
seen enough.

He cut the engine. They sat for a minute in silence, listening to the faint whistle and moan of the wind.

'Told you it had atmosphere,' he declared. He seemed stronger today, more vigorous altogether. Only once had she heard the gravelly cough.

They climbed down. Stones and masonry of all sizes, partially buried, poked up through the sand. She moved through them warily, her light canvas shoes sinking at each step. The hot sand quickly filled them.

'Careful now.' Larcum reached out to steady her as she stumbled. She drew back instinctively.

'It's OK . . . I should be helping you, I guess.'

He chuckled, shuffling forward beside her. They reached the big arch.

'Mind you,' he said, 'what you see here's barely half of it. Just part of the outer wall.' He gestured at the stones strewn about them, assuming the authority of the guide. 'Real rock, mind, not mud like Mohkran. The Merinides' slaves quarried out of these dunes . . .'

'Kind of grim for a palace.' She listened only vaguely, steeling herself for what must come.

'Ah. Mainly a prison, remember. The prisoners just happened to be royal . . .'

They mounted some half-exposed steps, walked through what remained of an upper level. To her it was simply dead stone. Twenty minutes and the tour was complete. All the while she kept him in sight, let him precede her. His trousers — slightly flared, deeply pressed — had clearly hung in his closet for years. Doubtless since the days he wore them to impress girls like her. Now they flapped loosely, held up by an oversized belt. For an instant she almost pitied him.

They stood near the entrance again — in what, she

assumed, had been a huge vestibule. She could feel her tension return.

Larcum sat down against a column, dabbing his face. It was rubicund now, and sweating.

'That accent of your's. I'm a stickler, you know . . . have to get things right. I've been listening hard. Idaho, Nebraska — am I right?'

Was this it? He smiled and all at once she imagined him asking Mo the same thing. Setting his quarry at ease. He was spot on, in fact, and she nodded. 'But that was way back.'

'I thought so!' He clapped his hands together, beaming. 'Right, time for refreshment, I think! White or red, my dear? ', he pushed himself up. 'The Médéa's not perhaps . . .'

She took a deep breath. 'Forget the wine, Larcum.'

He stopped and looked at her blankly.

'For Chrissake! You think we're here for a goddam *picnic*?'

His mouth gaped like an idiot's. 'I . . . I don't understand. Did I say something . . .?'

'Not a damn thing. You've *done* nothing, either! For twenty-nine years! That's just the fucking point!' The rage in her voice shook even her.

'Twenty-ni . . .? What is this, my dear? I'm not with you.'

'*Dear*? Why d'you keep calling me that? I thought you were *careful* with words?'

Still staring dumbly Larcum reached behind him, slumped back down.,

'As for "not with me" . . .' She gave a grunt of contempt. 'Have you *ever* been? You made promises, you bastard,' moving towards him now, 'so where were you, huh? Too busy lording it round Europe? Screwing other women? Or should that be *boys*?'

Her final remark seemed to fly clean by him. 'Promises?' he echoed, almost inaudibly.

Producing Mo's picture she thrust it at him. Limply he took it.

'Ring any bells? Go on, time you used those damn eyes!

He stared at the photo. Nodding, he said quietly: 'I *do* know this face . . .'

'Oh really?' she sneered. 'Go on, surprise me then.'

She tried to take back the picture, but he held it away from her.

'I mean, it's familiar from . . .' He looked slowly, light beginning to dawn. 'Twenty-nine years. Is it really?'

She stood in the sand as if frozen, continuing to watch him. He both revolted and fascinated her. 'So? Any names come to mind. Jo maybe? Jo-Anne? Jo-Anne Diedrickson. Still,' she added, 'I guess names came and went.'

'Wait a minute. You're not saying . . .' He held up the photo. 'This woman's your *mother*?'

She nodded.

'And you're suggesting . . . Oh, come now,' he chuckled nervously, 'that's preposterous!'

He was actually *laughing*! She thought suddenly of the knife in her bag. An overwhelming temptation rose in her to use it right now, cut short this charade. But that was too easy. She backed off, sat down on a rock, the bag on her knee. She dug her nails into her palms as he said:

'This woman . . . your mother—*she* told you this?'

'Amuses you, huh?'

'Now look. You're a bright woman, attractive . . . nothing would give me more pleasure than being your father. But believe me, that's impossible.'

'Oh yeah?'

He nodded. 'Regretably.'

'Christ,' she exclaimed, 'let me guess. Vasectomy, right? Or maybe it's impotence, huh? *Pff*! That's how you left her feeling all those years — impotent! It's how I've felt since I knew. Don't insult me, you bastard. I'm not buying your shit any longer!'

'Fine. In that case I need say nothing more.'

'You'd better. This story runs and you won't know what hit you.'

Sighing he pushed himself up, confronted her gravely. 'If a *word* of this lunacy appears — never mind medical details — I'll sue. Simple as that.' He held the stare. 'As you may know, TB can have certain . . . other effects. Anyway, it's not hard to verify. Hospital records. Might be wise to remember that.'

Just for an instant she wondered what it would mean were he telling the truth.

'OK, so do admit knowing her . . .'

Turning away from her Larcum lit up a cheroot. No holder this time. There was a pause before he said: 'It was thirty years ago, yes. A lecture tour, right across the States. I met, I imagine, *thousands* of people. The only reason I remember her is because she followed me. The whole way. Two bloody *months*, for heaven's sake! LA, Seattle, Chicago . . . each time I looked up — whatever hall or library or bookshop I was in — there she was. And when I'd finished a lecture, the reading — she always found some way to get to me. God,' he took a quick drag and exhaled, 'it's all coming back now. Hide-and-seek . . . all round America. Never been happier to leave, believe me. Vowed I'd never go back. She managed that single-handed. Quite an achievement.'

'And that's it?' Eve laughed bitterly. 'What you trying

to prove? That dumb plots still sell?' She stood up. 'You're despicable!' It was as if a magnet drew her toward him. With added impetus as Larcum retreated.

'Now listen . . .' he muttered.

'Oh-no. You're listening to me now.'

'Keep away . . .' He took another step back. 'Can't you *hear* what I'm telling you?'

He tripped suddenly on one of the stones, lost his balance. Toppled over with a stifled cry, arms and legs flailing. Trying to rise again from the sand he reminded her of a beetle stuck on its back. Raised on his elbows he tried to edge further back, but behind him was a wall. He sat up rigid against it as she came forward again and stood over him. His gaze seemed riveted to her side. She looked down, saw she was holding the knife.

'You don't change, do you? Even now. Always one more story.'

She crouched down, brought the blade to his cheek.

'Mo was nuts then? A stalker or something? That what you're saying?'

He sat frozen, eyes fixed on the knife.

'Like mother like daughter, huh? You think I'm crazy too?'

She felt almost high again, witnessing his terror. 'Jesus, I *knew* her!' She spoke low and intensely now, her face inches from his. 'Mo was *good*. An honest, good woman . . . a great mother. It's *you* who killed her! With *grief*! Disappointment. Yeah, you think about it, Larcum.'

She stood up sharply and turned away, caught between weeping and murderous anger.

Her back was still toward him when he let out a sharp yelp. She wheeled round. Dangling from his hand, its tail arched back into the flesh, hung a sizeable scorpion.

Temporarily stunned, she watched him try to shake

the thing free, but the scorpion clung stubbornly on. Eve struggled to recall what Mati had told her, what one should do. Larcum, too, appeared in shock. Then, as the creature dropped suddenly to the dust and scuttled away, he clutched the hand against him, began rocking like someone with stomach cramps, moaning quietly.

'For pity's sake, woman . . .' Sweat beaded his forehead. His eyes were creased and leaky with pain. 'Help me . . .'

But she stood there, immobile, watching him numbly.

'What the hell do you want?' Larcum gasped. 'Apologies?' His breath was shorter now. 'OK, OK, I'm sorry,' he muttered, still rocking. 'Mohkan . . . Dr Ibrahim . . . quickly . . .'

'Quit whining, OK? I'm trying to *think* here!'

She looked at him lolling there, mouth hanging open.

'What you saying?' she asked sharply. 'It'll *kill* you?'

She couldn't tell if he nodded or whether it was involuntary movement. He seemed to be losing it fast. She went over and shook him. 'For Chrissake, Larcum. Answer me.'

'Fat-tail . . . lethal . . . two, three hours . . .' He continued to murmur but to her it was gibberish.

'We have to get to the jeep,' she said, pulling him up. He stank of sweat now, rambling, legs almost gone. 'Jesus, man—you gotta help yourself here!'

She got his good arm round her shoulders. All his weight was against her, pulling them down. Slowly, pausing every few feet, she dragged him forward through the stones. Out of the last welcome shadow, into the blaze of the sun. The trail they left was a snake-like zig-zag in the sand. It seemed to take forever but at last they were back at the vehicle.

Even then it took all her strength to get him up through

the door, fold him into the passenger seat. The heat was unreal. Groggy, gasping for breath, she lifted the tailgate, snapped free the lid of the cold-box. There were two tall bottles of mineral water next to the wine, foiled parcels of food packed around them. Gulping down most of one bottle she sat there, listening to Larcum ramble, striving to order her thoughts till some measure of equilibrium returned. Then she went round to the driver's side and climbed in.

'Here, drink some of this.'

She held the bottle steady. He appeared to have revived a little, was clearly avid for water, though most dribbled from the sides of his mouth. She wondered if paralysis had already set in, or whether it was still largely shock. She fired up the engine and pulled slowly away, following the tracks they had made coming in.

It was almost midday but the air had grown hazy, yellowish: a fine gauze of sand blew diagonally across them. She hunched forward close to the screen. Before long the glass was streaky with dust: she flicked on the wipers but to little effect. Her ability to rationalise seemed equally impaired; even switching gear required conscious effort. After a while she decided to hold it in second, crawling forward, searching for the next marker.

She could've just left him of course, driven back alone. In a way, what could've been more perfect? She could have wept convincingly, explain how she'd panicked, thought it best that help came to him. Some would blame her, think her a fool, but nothing could stick. Most would be thankful that one of them had made it.

Larcum remained incoherent beside her. His head lolled heavily with each jolt, his thin white hair lank with sweat.

'*Shsssh* . . .quiet now,' she said. 'It's not long from

here.' She stepped on the gas and moved up into third. The highway was another few kilometres.

Him or Mo: one of them had lied. She realised that never before had she questioned anything Mo told her. Anything *about* her. Not seriously. What she did or said; her intelligence; her love.

Suddenly all she could see through the screen was dust, a dense swirling cloud. Braking instinctively, she felt the jeep lurch and spin. She struggled with the wheel as they slewed sideways and on, thudded into and over something; were finally still.

'Dammit,' she breathed.

She looked quickly across at Larcum and thrust the drive into reverse. The wheels whirred and spun beneath her, the smell of burnt fuel filled the air, but the jeep failed to move. She swore again, banged the wheel in frustration and got out.

They'd skidded a surprising distance, right off the piste. The front wheels were bogged to the axles.

In the back was a shovel, across the roof-rack a pair of sand-ladders. After barely five minutes, however, she knew her efforts were futile. Other than forcing the ladders still deeper into the holes she had dug, the four-wheel gear-shift served no discernible purpose. Finally, bent almost double next to the vehicle, she gave one weak kick at the tyre and threw the spade aside.

Dark patches of sweat stained Larcum's shirt. He was silent now, almost comatose. She loosened more of his buttons, restarted the engine so the air-conditioner came on, then searched for his pulse. It was there, but faint. She placed what remained of the water beside him, reached for her bag and slipped the other, full bottle inside.

'Wish us luck,' she said, with a last look across.

She closed the door, pulled on her hat and started to

walk — head down, hugging the bag to her. Her mouth and nostrils were soon gritty and parched. She stopped and drank. Looking back the jeep was barely visible now: a tiny, shimmering point between the huge ochre dunes.

Replacing the bottle she noticed the goat-hide sheath, the knife still there in her bag. Lifting it out she turned it in her hand for a moment, then hurled it as far as she could, out into the sand.

Even now she was uncertain — once she reached the highway, provided someone came by — which way she hoped they were heading.

Borderline

'LIKE FLOATY, SMILED Amar, his face held up to the sun. He let his arms drift wide in the swell. 'That firss time, *tuan* . . . never have I known such feeling.'

Hurst trod water and watched him. Carefree. Untroubled. Could what he said be believed? More likely, Hurst thought, the sun had affected them both. All day its glare had bounced from the water, stabbing his eyes till they ached. Even recalling how he came to be here — chestdeep in the South China Sea — for a moment defeated him. And why should a stranger wish to tell him these things?

Turning, he swam strongly for the shore. He could see their two towels, tiny islands of colour marooned on the sand. Once he reached them he lay down and closed his eyes. The heat bore into him, the droplets of water evaporating from his skin. At length he sat up, found his dark glasses and opened his book — *Speak Malay!*

Propped on an elbow, he tried to recall everything Amar had told him. It was tempting to believe he had misunderstood, that language divided them. But he knew it wasn't so. He looked up, watched the sleek buoyant shape in the water. Like a seal in its element. By sharing his secret, Amar appeared to have shed its weight. Transferred it, for sure, since Hurst felt a new sense of burden. Privately he'd nursed a certain pride in his own self-effacement, his readiness to listen. Now, not for the first time lately, he began to regret it.

Amar was calling him, laughing. 'Come, *tuan*! Swimmy! Is good!'

Wearily Hurst raised an arm but made no effort to move. Instead he rolled over, looked up the shore.

It was a weekday, granted, but still the emptiness of the beach seemed remarkable. He made out only one other couple, some distance along the tidal ridge. The tropical light was generous to the sand, flattened and obscured its litter and driftwood to a uniform, brochure-clean pallor. For when he'd arrived, soon after dawn, the usual detritus had been all too apparent from the primitive bar beneath the palms. Hurst screwed up his eyes, strained to distinguish it from the treeline's deep shadow. He'd walked the short distance from the bus to where the road became sand . . . paused at the counter and asked for a beer.

Just a few hours. It felt days ago already. The old man had come shuffling across with a bottle of Anchor. Things were still simple then, he reflected. The murmur of the surf; a nearby beach-hut creaking on its stilts; now and then the stallholder's fly-swat thwacking the counter.

'*Tuan*?'

Hurst started, turned on his side. Amar stood over him, black hair dripping. His wet skin seemed darker than ever, a glossy smoothness that was almost surreal. His smile broadened, the nascent moustache lifted a little. A face like the moon, thought Hurst. And as difficult to read.

'You no liking me now?' Amar brought the towel over his head, rubbing it in a half-hearted, childlike way. '*Tuan*? he repeated.

'Amar, please. I know it's habit, a mark of respect, but . . . no more *tuan*. OK?'

The smile faltered. '*Minta ampun*. I forget. Is Ton-ee, yes?'

'Tony, that's right.'

Amar dropped to his knees in the sand, sat back. 'I bad man to tell you this thing. You no more my fren.'

'It's not true,' Hurst said, looking beyond him to the empty sea. 'Anyway, I think I understand now. That's just as important.'

The evening before, once the mosquitoes had driven him from the rest-house verandah, he'd spread his map on the bed and tried to summon an interest in the day to come. His visa for Thailand was still being processed; it meant another day kicking his heels. Tracing the line of the coast his finger paused briefly at a number of places — Pantai Cinta Berahi among them — but passed quickly on. The Beach of Passionate Love. Hyperbole for the tourists, another dreamed-up legend. Obvious and off-putting. Since Kate and he finished, moreover, most allusions to love left him cynical, bitter.

So why had his finger edged back?

As if vaguely ashamed, he'd slipped away early and taken the bus. The beach was a few miles north of Kota Bharu; without the stamp in his passport he could go little further in any case. Several times during the day he'd found himself peering down the ribbon of shore, wondering where Thailand began. Perhaps there, finally, he could exhume this deadness that remained inside, bury it for good before the plane took him back. He could only face the new term as the start of a separate life. And he still wasn't ready.

For hours he'd stared at the sea or half-listened to Amar, thinking like this. The whole journey he saw now for what it was. Ill-conceived. Pointless. As long as memory travelled with one—it was compulsory luggage, after all—then how could it be otherwise?

He'd just finished the beer when Amar arrived. Despite his native features he was dressed like a tourist himself: frayed shorts, flip-flops, Rolling Stones T-shirt. A solid but well-toned figure, the chopped sleeves and shorts displaying prominent muscles. Having greeted one another he settled at a neighbouring bench and called for a large jug of water. This set the old man muttering—something about Chinese tight-fistedness from what Hurst could fathom—though in due course the jug did appear. Upon which the newcomer downed four straight glasses with barely a pause.

'Please, no worry,' Amar had beamed, catching Hurst's glance. 'Sun steal water quick!' His eye fell on the bottle of beer, empty now. 'Anchor no good, sir!' He shook his head gravely.

Hurst assumed he spoke as a Muslim teetotaler. One could take it as read that most Malays—in particular from the ultra-orthodox north—had Mohammedan inscribed on their documents. 'I'm sorry,' he began, 'I hope you don't . . .'

The man threw back his head, laughing heartily. 'You drink please. No sin for you, yes? But beer make you sweat . . . sweat bad, *tuan* . . . make brain going soft. Please, I only advice.'

So their day had begun.

Hurst might have had difficulty pinning him down had Amar proved less forthcoming. His *name* was Islamic of course; but judged by manner and dress—outgoing, Westernised, confident; not to mention his roundness of face and the stallholder's bitter aside—Amar had to be partly Chinese. Whatever the truth, though, it would clearly reveal itself. Amar liked to talk and to begin with

Hurst found himself content to let the words wash over him. Any diversion from his brooding was welcome.

Amar was a Customs officer, employed at the nearby post. Today, Monday, was his day-off. He had a passion for swimming and often came to this beach.

'And what work you?' he'd asked.

Hurst was tempted to make something up. Anything but teacher. His companion seemed delighted, however.

'Ah, this Amar lucky day, sir! Now you teach me new Ingriss words. Malay School vey bad. Chinese they teach nothing. Is true.' He stood, lifted his blunt nose in the air. 'Come, *tuan*. All sea it await us!' He looked across, beaming. They picked up their things and set off towards the water. Already the sand was warm underfoot.

'It's always this quiet?'

'No-no!' Amar frowned. 'This famous beach. Someday many peoples. Today we *both* lucky!'

Briefly, around midday, a group of office workers materialised from nowhere, twenty or so, identically clad in dark suits. Two points of commotion soon developed: one round the food stall, the other at the water's edge. Hurst sat up to watch. Shortly most were lining the benches, shovelling rice to their bent-over faces. The rest — trousers rolled to the knee but still wearing ties and starched shirts — splashed and paddled like kids out of school.

He must have dozed at some point for when he looked again the long curve of sand shimmered peacefully. He and Amar talked and swam on alone, let the sun burn them before swimming again.

Amar came from the south, Johor Bahru, the last city before Singapore. He'd been up here six years now — and that was enough.

'Nex month I go back. For long time I counting ees

day. Many fren in Johor. Work better also. Big house, many ringgit.'

'Ah, promotion.'

They lay in the shallows, let the water wash round them.

'Pro..mosh..? Aya! *Naik prangkat* we say. Some good thing I mus leave here . . .' Regret flickered momentarily. 'But the girrs in Johor! You see them, *tuan*? No *purdah*, no veil. An so pretty!'

Amar's eyes closed. He joined his hands behind his head and lay back. Foam ebbed at his side. 'You marry, sir?'

Hurst knew it was coming but he had no response. Answering yes (though strictly still true) seemed to invite complication. Not long ago he would have lied without thought—to save, as he believed, time or pain. Whereas now he knew how the simplest omission could snowball. Anyway, he'd had enough of explaining, to himself or to anyone else. Amar opened one eye and looked at him. When Hurst failed to answer he rolled over, sat up.

'Oh, but . . .' His mouth hung open. 'But you hansum man. An Ingriss girrs they . . .'

Hurst was conscious of Amar's gaze playing over him. Fool, he berated himself, looking away. Their isolation, Amar's attentiveness, had been nagging him from the start, but only now did he realise. He couldn't rid himself of the impression that this meeting had been somehow arranged. Though that was ridiculous, naturally. He turned and their eyes met for an instant, held one another. Up this close, Amar's seemed flat and lifeless as mirrors. Without breaking the silence Hurst got to his feet. Strode to the waterline and waded back out.

As though reading his mind, Amar followed quickly, splashing in beside him. 'I like . . . *tuan*, I like vey much the white girrs. They no hiding face. No shames. One day I hope . . . some like Chinee-boy you think maybe?'

The same distance was there in his gaze when he spoke again of the south, of his family. Not quite nostalgia, Hurst thought. Nor love, not really. The longer they talked the more Amar's bearing, his romantic self-image, suggested delusion. Above all he appeared conscious of the limits of his life. Hurst saw this quite clearly — an empathy which surprised him.

Since coming north, Amar had lived in a small local *kampung* — not far from his post at the border. This village he described variously as isolated, backward, tiny . . . without even a name on the map. Despite every disclaimer, however (*People no clean . . . many thief . . . my home no water no letrik*) his love for the place was self-evident. To Hurst too it sounded perversely ideal, somewhere he could lose himself happily while he waited. Aloud he admitted it. But Amar leapt at once on any hint of charm.

'*Petani* vey stupid. White face make them afraid! Is true. Some try an touch you maybe. Other run away . . .'

To Hurst, however, it sounded increasingly attractive.

'But no worry, sir — they my fren. Later I show, yes? Great honour to me. You will stay Amar room . . .?'

Hurst felt inclined to accept while the offer remained. Certainly it promised an episode as intriguing as *wayang kulit* — the shadow-play he'd planned to witness this evening in town. Doubts still nagged him, however. Amar's ambiguous gaze. The unidentified village. And would thieves or smugglers tolerate a customs man as their neighbour, even off-duty?

But Amar was grinning now. The idea had seized him and wouldn't let go. The hut was simple, he continued. Only one bed ('I sleeping on mat, no problem'), bucket shower out back. 'Also my excise thing there. But them I moving, OK?'

It took an accompanying mime for Hurst to deduce he meant exercise, nothing to do with his work. Body-building; weights; one of those bikes. Which explained his physique.

Of course, Amar confided (floating easily beside him), he could have opted for government quarters — rent-free, appropriate to his status. But to do so entailed longer contracts. The remark reemphasised his view of the region: to him it was a social and cultural wasteland. He seemed anxious that the years spent away from Johore had indelibly marked him, would set him apart upon his return. Though ostensibly he dismissed such ideas.

'Soon I frisk Singapore bag! Eat bes Canton meal, see thousan nice lady . . .!'

'Really?' Hurst observed, seeing a chance to clarify things. 'What's The Prophet say about that? The ladies?'

Amar returned his smile. Until two years ago, he responded obliquely, he'd prepared like his brothers for the ultimate pilgrimage, the Haj.

'My mother she Buddhis Chinese. See,' he pointed, 'this her nose! Same ugly face! But Ibn Saïd — my father, yes? — he Arab blood. Raise three son by Q'ran. Eas day we pray in Mosque Abu Bakar. When Ibn Saïd he die I promis I be pilgrim like him, make journey to Ka'aba, kiss the black stone. Then I too will be Haji! Haji Amar bin Ibn Saïd!' His smile dimmed momentarily. 'But for this I need many dollar. Four, five year I save Custom money . . .'

Then, not long ago, two men approached the border while Amar was on duty. Like many who passed at this crossing they were backpackers, young, moving south from Bangkok. These happened to be Swiss.

'They in big hurry . . .' (again Hurst noted the ambivalent smile) 'I say sure, check quick an you go. But look inside bag an it lie there, no hidden. *Hasis*, yes? They have *paip* also . . . little pipe. Some peoples they no smuggle good!'

He gleamed with pride, bobbing on the current.

'Is lucky for them. Find heroin, big drug, judge say you hang. But *hasis* still trouble. Lock-up Penang or KL . . . bad prison long time.'

He ducked under with scarcely a ripple, let himself sink. Hurst trod water and waited. Half-a-minute elapsed, maybe more. Irritation turned to alarm: he was about to dive down when a dark outline — wavy, ill-defined — took shape close beside him. An instant later, sleek as ever, it broke to the surface. Cheeks puffed, Amar shook his hair with exuberance, lay back and blew a fine spray skyward.

'For Chrissake!' Hurst exclaimed. 'Stop clowning about. If drowning's what you want then wait till I've gone, OK?'

Amar looked at him blankly. His disbelief, even hurt, appeared genuine. And Hurst couldn't explain such an outburst. He heard the echo of his petulant, schoolmaster's voice — the professional rebuker — and loathed himself for it.

'I've swum enough for one day,' he said.

He wasn't concerned whether Amar would follow. Reaching his depth his feet touched the bottom. His torso was clear of the water now but still the tide's weight held him back. Trying to move quicker he lost his balance, stumbled forward into the surf. As he struggled to rise a small breaker struck his back with unexpected power, forcing him down again. At which point he felt a sudden rush of panic. A memory of Kate had come flashing before

him, the same sense of floundering he'd felt as she clung
to him, that final evening. Sobbing explanations while
he strove to break free. No, not so much panic as shame.
Shame and regret . . .

But then he was standing again. He climbed clear of
the water and up the small slope, breathing heavily.

By the time Amar joined him he felt somewhat
calmer. To avoid raising his eyes he picked up the tube
of Solaire, applied some with studied concentration. And
before Amar could speak he asked: 'What happens once
you catch them? Right afterwards, I mean. Ones like the
Swiss.'

In truth he was not greatly interested, it was simply a
diversion away from himself. Amar hunched sheepishly
over his toes, brushing sand from between them. His
lower lip jutted like a sulking child's. 'Maybe is better
. . .' His voice trailed away. 'Tonee . . . why I tell you
this thing?'

His sigh was so out of character that Hurst almost
laughed. 'Who knows?' After a moment he said: 'I'd like
to hear though. Honestly.'

Amar frowned with confusion. Nonetheless he
resumed.

'I take to room we use private. For strip search. I ask
them: "Why you try fool me? This Amar job, he smart
man."' A tentative smile. '"Look," I say, "ev'rywhere
warning what happen to smuggler. Why then you do
this?"'

Naked, arms splayed to the wall, the first Swiss tried
to explain as Amar's hands went to work. Though the
situation was beyond Hurst's experience the clarity of the
picture cut through his initial indifference. Michel and
Pièrre. Amar recalled the men's names without hesitation.

To him, it appeared, the episode might have been only yesterday.

'Mishal he say: "Of *course* we no traffik. Is personal use only. To make us feel good."'

Conversation, too, he seemed to be quoting verbatim, his mouth touched by a smile now. Despite the subject, a kind of eagerness lit up his face. It was this more than anything that Hurst found disquieting.

' "Say here you both marry," ' Amar continued, reenacting his scrutiny of the passports. ' "Where your womans?" '

' "In Genève we have wife," say Mishal. He more frighten than Per, he talk more. But hot place they no like . . . make them sick. Long journey same. They go ski, stay in mountain. "Some holiday," he say, "is Per an me only." ' Amar smiled broadly. 'Is funny these men, you think?'

Hurst made no reply.

'Then Mishal laugh an he say: "We promis wife no naughty girrs when we gone. An we always keep promise. But three, four week . . . is hard sometime, yes? Without woman. So, we make party ourself, only we two. You un'erstan now, custom man?" '

He broke off. His look, Hurst decided, now asked the same question of him. To his continuing silence Amar reacted with a scowl of frustration. Suddenly Hurst knew that he'd told this story before; to other men, perhaps on this same strip of beach.

'*Tuan*?'

'Amar, look . . .'

'Please to forgive . . . I not say again.' A pause before he added: 'You think Amar ugly? Like Chinee mother? Please, Tonee . . . speak true to me now.'

Momentarily Hurst looked away. He found the

hangdog gaze, the suppliant tone embarrassing. But when he turned back Amar still stared at him in a way which made Hurst deeply uncomfortable. He felt rising anger without knowing why. What did Amar see in him, to induce such misapplied awe? Pale hair thinning on top . . . a long nose . . . blotchy skin unused to the heat. Just the things, in fact, he most disliked in himself. Even through a foreigner's eyes he couldn't imagine such features as appealing. 'We're all ugly,' he replied. 'It's not always visible, that's all.' He felt hot and tired, wanted one final swim after all. 'Are you coming?'

Only briefly did the water feel cool. And as soon as they were in it Amar pressed on. 'I say to this Mishal: "No. I no un'erstan. How you mean? Please show." They look at me like I crazy. Per he shake bad now. He ask "You are serious?" an because in this time I know nothing I say "Sure. You show please."'

'So they fill their *paip* an I look. Mishal say again, "Is inn'cent, see? We smoke only together, like this. To discover the mood, to relax. Is making us happy . . ." They pass pipe an smile . . . not quite easy, you know. They say, "You try also. You un'erstan then."'

'You think is bad thing I do, Tonee, yes? You think Allah watch an he punish?'

'Is that how it works? Don't you call him All-Merciful?'

Amar smiled. 'Some things Qur'an does not speak of. From that day I know this. I want only to learn . . . to open the eyes, yes? But then this smoke make me strainsh. How can I say . . . vey happy, no worry. I see Per an Mishal together like this . . .'

Amar bobbed closer. Treading water he opened one hand, held it flat, just clear of the surface. Slowly from above he lowered the other till the two palms were touching.

'Face face, yes? There on floor. Is so strainsh how I feel when I see this . . .' Amar's eyes were half-closed. The dreamy half-smile had returned. For a moment Hurst watched the two hands move lightly against one another. Then Amar lay back and was floating.

'Looking make me feel good . . . this body so light . . . like Ramadan end. I see an I know I mus do this . . .'

Bar the rawness of his shoulders, the salt water licking them, Hurst felt almost insensible. The sun had drained him of energy. Once more Amar's words were breaking over him like the tide. What use are customs anyway, he thought vaguely. Without them — one way and another — today would have been very different.

'I send Mishal to washroom then I tell Per: "All hash I burn now. Save you long prison . . . ten year maybe. For this I ask only one thing." An Per he jus smile. He touch me an say: 'Is bes deal we have . . .'

Almost imperceptibly the current had carried them. Hurst noticed their towels on the shore, some distance away now. 'I must go,' he announced, cutting through what Amar was saying:

'We lie same as he an Mishal — face face . . .'

Recumbent, round-bellied, legs and arms stirring lazily in the clear greenish water. Their outline distorted, trembling.

'. . . an again comes this feeling, not like with woman. With woman is like drowning, yes, but this . . . this is *free*. You know?'

The sea clung like liquid glass. Amar's words seemed to come from somwhere beyond him. A breeze ruffled the water and Hust knew at last just what his fear was.

That somehow it was *them*, him and Amar, in that airless back-room.

He looked up. Colour was seeping back to the sky. Along the horizon steep towers of cloud gathered. He thought of last night, the night before that: rain hammering the guest-house roof, pouring in streams from the gutters.

'And since then?' he asked, knowing the answer already. Of course there'd been others. Dozens, probably. That was the point.

'Sure, many take risk, try clever thing. But always I ask if they want. Most say, "After this we both are forgetting, OK?" '

'And women . . . women smugglers? They interest you too?'

Amar chuckled, raising a small wash around him. 'You funny man! Two time I try girrs. Is diff'ren I think. But soon in Johor . . . maybe there I find girr make it good. Like with Per, like floaty. That firss time, *tuan* . . . never have I known such feeling . . .'

So Hurst had swum strongly for the beach, their two bright towels marooned on the ridge. Behind his glasses he watched Amar float on. Grains of sand collected in the leaves of his book. He dredged his memory for all that had passed between them. The red sun fell and in the course of time Amar stood over him, his wet body dripping. His smile wavered when he fell to his knees, said again, 'I bad man I tell you this thing. You no more my fren.'

And Hurst stared beyond him to the empty sea.

'It's not true. Anyway, I think I understand now. That's just as important.'

Now Amar sat beside him, cross-legged on the towel.

'I have no way to live if . . . if you . . . I lose job, my fam'ly. This big secret, yes?'

'Don't worry. Why should I speak of it? Who is there to tell?'

Even as he spoke he knew it had a hollow ring. Secrets—if secret it was—respected no boundaries, were invariably smuggled on.

'Tonee listen.' Hurst started as Amar touched his arm. 'Is not like you think. One boy he from Sydney . . . we keeping good fren, write letter. His name Greg. Two time he come visit, stay in my *kampung*. Greg he say: "This way you lose hang-up."—Is right, yes? Hang-up? He say: "Since with Mishal and Per you new man . . . *happy* man!" He say is good no more Q'ran, no shames. Is true you think, Tonee?'

Hurst looked north along the shore. A sort of haze had formed: purplish, iridescent.

They dressed in silence, rolled up the towels. Darkness came quickly here—day then night, nothing between. Climbing the beach he felt weak, his bare feet sunk in the sand. They approached the *kedai*: the counter was shuttered, the shopkeeper gone. Mosquitoes hummed invisibly under the trees. Moving to the bus-stop they stood a while before Amar repeated his request.

'Come village,' he said.

Hurst peered down the avenue of white eucalyptus, their trunks like ghosts in the dusk. He couldn't see the bus yet, though somewhere he believed he could hear it—rattling distantly through the potholes. His thoughts were confused. He tried hard to picture the brigandish neighbours. He saw a room with rush matting . . . an exercise bike. The one narrow bed.

'Promis no trouble,' came Amar's voice. 'I look after you good.'

His face was scarcely visible but Hurst knew it was smiling. For some reason he also believed him.

As he lifted his hold-all, slung it over his shoulder, the rattle-trap slewed into sight, came clattering toward them with its lights bouncing drunkingly. Together they watched it approach. Against the feeble glow from inside Hurst made out one or two figures, a face pressed to a window.

Then he turned and was saying: 'Honestly, Amar, I can't. Don't ask me to explain. I just . . .' He shrugged. 'I'm going back to the shadow-play.'

With absurd formality he held out his hand. The bus swung round beside them, scraping its gears, and lurched to a halt.

The Wood Yard

UNTIL THIS SUMMER I half-believed Montazeau didn't exist.

Down shady and deserted roads I'd come across signs that said otherwise, but despite several detours had never tracked it down. On the map the junctions where such clues exist form a sort of box round a deep wooded area—the Forêt de la Chasse. Marked within it is a sizeable lake and a few scattered hamlets. But none to correspond with the signs by the road.

It was a puzzle. Perhaps, though, I never looked seriously enough. Preferred it a mystery. In any event, only chance seemed likely to provide a solution.

I'd forgotten about the *mobylette*—it had been there so long, gathering dust in the tool-shed. But no sooner had we arrived than Karen discovered it. I heard the shed door creak and when she re-entered the house and found me unpacking—even before she said: 'Why, you old humbug!'—I detected a twinkle of revenge in her smile and guessed at its cause.

'All this time . . .' she laughed, pointing outside. 'Acting so superior while that's sitting out there! Go on, talk your way out of this!'

I sighed and said, 'Very well.' Tired of her nonsense and trusting it would end here. 'One, it's not a bicycle. Two, I've never ridden it. And three . . .' I hesitated. 'It belonged to my son.'

She sat slowly down on the bed. Unsurprisingly, this had silenced even her. I continued to arrange my shirts in the drawer. Finally she said without looking up: 'I can't take much more of this, Paul. Why won't you *tell* me things? What are you afraid of? Your *son*, for God's sake. And you talk as though he were . . .'

'He is,' I said. 'There, now you know two things.'

I left the room then.

Some days passed, not unpleasant ones. We drove out to the coast and swam. Afterwards in the dunes was agreeable. In that regard Karen retains her invention. Most mornings we took in a market.

The subject was still on our minds though. I could sense her deciding how best to return to it. And one night at dinner—we were at La Terrasse, overlooking the river—she said out of nowhere, 'At least let me clean the thing, Paul,' aware no further reference was needed. 'I can't stand to see it like that, it's not right.'

When I didn't reply she went on:

'Otherwise sell it. You can't mourn for ever . . . if that's what you're doing. We could trade it in for a couple of bikes. It's so *beautiful* here . . . You might even enjoy it.'

She disappointed me seriously, resurrecting this bone of contention. All I seek is equanimity—a quiet life on my own terms. Anyway, I'm told I still belie my years and, as a matter of principle, have no intention of taking up exercise now.

Karen, however, cycles everywhere—even in London. Her assertion that to do so is quicker and less stressful than travelling by car did briefly amuse me. Idiosyncrasies can be affecting and, despite what some claim, I'm a tolerant man. I must confess, too, that her excellent legs were my first focus of attention. That was two years ago, when her bike wobbled out of Austin Street and drew alongside us at the lights. In a strangely impulsive moment I merely wound down the window. A few seconds later she rode off with my card.

Still, her claims were so insistent, so patently absurd, that some months later I finally tired and challenged her for proof. The next morning we set out for the City in tandem: Groves and myself in the Daimler, Karen pedaling. The outcome was hardly in doubt of course, and Groves is a wonder when it comes to short-cuts. As predicted we arrived fresh as two daisies; followed, some four minutes later, by Karen — breathless and glistening. All fairly conclusive.

She took it badly, sulking for days. But it seemed the point had been made. For some while she made no further effort to hijack my health. (Or do I mean my life?) She started riding the tube into work — a new PA job I'd helped to arrange — but after hours she was soon pedaling away again, perspiring ecstatically, tiresomely voluble about 'restored bio-rhythms'.

Let's be clear: I'm all for both sexes looking and feeling their best. It would be disingenuous to pretend that I share no interest in this. No, it's Karen's self-conviction, her unquenchable optimism that gets to me. Makes me fear for her too. London traffic, we all know, is no docile or predictable beast and life is fragile enough without exposing oneself unnecessarily. On a bike what chance has one got? Other considerations aside, a man in my position could never afford to be so vulnerable.

Karen hadn't seen the French house before. It's the first time, in fact, that I've brought anyone with me. These weeks away are precious, I've always protected them closely. Perhaps age is finally stalking me, however. Sentiment, fear of loneliness. I don't know.

As we came south, reached the neighbouring valleys

and vineyards, I could see the landscape seducing her. It should've pleased me, but my heart began to sink. I drew her attention to the gradients we struggled up, already half-resigned. Any day I anticipated the launch of another campaign — only this time what response could I give? Out here, she'd say, one was meant to act differently, to relax. I'd call it 'lowering one's guard.' But how could I argue these lanes held a threat?

I heard all this in her voice at La Terrasse and next morning found myself walking up to the village with a card for the shop window: MOBYLETTE Á VENDRE. Karen could be highly compliant once she got her own way, but even this no longer consoled me. Things had to change. This issue concerning the moped, the unanswered questions I read in her eyes about Jamie, the past . . . her curiosity wouldn't be still. Some weeks ago I thought I'd made clear the parameters — the day I came home and discovered her in my study. She made her excuses, hurried out, but there on the desk, where I never leave documents unattended, was the bill of sale for Liberia. How much she took in, I can't say; hopefully not enough to know its value or how to make use of it. Still, nothing is certain. I should have acted more decisively then.

The *épicerie* was quiet. I filled a basket with tomatoes, artichokes, goat's cheese — enough for our immediate needs — then made my enquiry, handing the card to the girl on the till. The customer behind me ventured an opinion: so-and-so, the butcher's young cousin, would buy it. Not at that price, put in another. Before I knew it, further pundits had drifted in off the street, drawn like flies by the animated discussion. Shortly the till was surrounded, a gesticulating bedlam. At which point I made for the door.

'*Attendez, m'sieur!*,' called a red-faced barrel of a

woman, emerging from the rabble with my card, beaming like a bridesmaid with the bouquet. '*Blaise, ce mec ici . . .*' she fussed, printing details on the reverse, '*il est marchand des ces choses. Un bricoleur, comprenez?*' A fixer.

'*Son télèphone ne marche jamais,*' she babbled on, handing the card back. 'Just take the 'moby' to him. He's always there, tinkering.'

I dropped the card in the bag and exited hastily, anxious only for peace.

Leaving the groceries in the kitchen—Karen was preparing a salad—I went down to the cellar for some claret. I needed to think and a good wine helps. Back upstairs I was drawing the cork when she called from next door:

'Who's Pascal?'

Her interest surprised me. 'Dead philosopher,' I muttered, filling a glass. 'The best kind.'

'So why's his address . . .?' A pause. 'Ohh, Paul, you sweetie. You did it.' She appeared in the doorway. 'When are we going?'

I looked up, saw the card in her hand. 'Ah,' I smiled faintly. 'Him. That's really his name?'

She nodded. 'Blaise Pascal. Le Boucher, Montazeau. Where's that?'

I had turned away to set out the plates. Montazeau? I went over and took the card from her casually, beginning to tingle. She knew nothing of my goose-chase over the years and I wasn't about to broach it with her now. But finally I might have an answer.

'You mean *Le Bûcher*, dearest,' I corrected her, reading. 'The woodshed. You said he was a butcher!'

That shed, the idea of a woodyard, at least gave Montazeau a hint of identity. For the first time I began to imagine it not a village at all, in some way just part of the forest. I recalled the muffled buzzing of chainsaws one always heard in that region.

Pocketing the card, I poured her a glass. 'Quick bite and we'll go. How's that?'

She looked almost stunned for an instant; then pecked at my cheek and turned away happily. I pondered further while laying the table.

Afterwards, armed with duster and polish, Karen wheeled the machine into the garden. Wanting as little as possible to do with the matter—it felt like an exhumation—I went round and checked the oil in the Volvo. Lowered the seats and spread out a groundsheet. Once she'd done we lifted the machine in together. Like his coffin, I thought. Leaving for burial.

There are several roads to choose from. I took the one across the ridge. We drove largely in silence but next to me I could sense her excitement—she gave it off with her body-heat. We climbed over the top to where the hairpins begin. They took us down steeply, a series of switchbacks, into the trees. I saw a boy walking a dog and pulled in to ask further directions. When we drove on Karen said: 'Isn't there a shorter way?'

I glanced across at her, thinking I caught an edge of mistrust. But she simply had the map on her knee, attempting to trace with her finger. As lost and confused as I'd been up to now.

'Put it away. I know where I'm going.' It still wasn't true, not exactly, but I wanted her head up, to note the route we were taking.

Even as we passed I failed to see any sign. It was Karen who called out: 'There—that was it! Back up!'

I reversed about thirty yards. Felled trunks were stacked like great walls on both sides of the track.

'See?' She pointed through her open window. The

word was daubed in red paint, one letter per log-face, midway up the wall: M-O-N-T-A-Z-E-A-U. And some arrows >>>>> pointing into the woods.

I had to smile. Even this definitive proof must come and go with the timber. Tomorrow the place could be nameless again. Unfindable.

We bumped along slowly, the baked ruts carpeted with shavings, pine needles, cones. After several hundred metres the track opened out in a dust-white clearing, doubtless where the lorries were loaded. A cabinless trailer and hoist rested on blocks by the tree-line; otherwise the space was deserted. An intermittent tapping, metal on metal, emanated from the open door of a long low cabin, its corrugated roof green with moss. The sound echoed round the clearing.

I got the *mobylette* out of the car myself, wheeled it forward and parked it in the shade by the doorway. Karen followed me in.

The office was empty. Led by the hammering we walked through to the back and down some steps. A shirtless man was working in a lean-to, bent over a disembow-eled engine. Swarthy, tousle-haired, a sweat-darkened handkerchief tied at his neck.

I explained what we had and were looking for. He wiped his oil-covered hands on a rag and led us back through to inspect the machine. Mid-afternoons business was quiet, Pascal told us. That's when he repaired things. Whatever people brought him.

'*Ah oui, c'est classique,*' he declared, stroking the chrome that Karen had worked on. I looked away at his rack of second-hand cycles and proposed an exchange:

'*Les bicyclettes, monsieur. On fait un marché?*'

'*Mais bien sûr. Suivez-moi.*'

The transaction was swift. I let Karen select: hers some

new-fangled lightweight, a racer; mine more conventional. Both seemed in excellent order. I handed over a few francs, the balance agreed. We bade the fellow goodbye and left him to his hammering.

Fitting two bikes in the back of an estate is not, of course, difficult. These were good as new though, and deliberately I'd brought no blankets or padding, nor straps for the roof. In short I fussed around for a while, puffing a little, cursing under my breath — till Karen's impatience was tangible. Her anxiety about damaging the machines, coupled with her eagerness to be riding again, convinced me I had only to delay long enough. Indeed, it took less time than I bargained for.

'For heaven's sake!' she exclaimed. 'This is ridiculous. We've got them to use! Come on, fetch mine out.'

I stared at her nonplussed, as doubtless she expected. She was mad, I repeated. Hadn't she *noticed* those hills? 'And you'll never remember the way . . .'

At which point she pushed me aside. It was now safe to demur. The decision was hers.

'Well,' I said, 'at least let me give you a start. I'll catch you up on the ridge. Make sure you . . .'

'Huh, you'll be lucky!' Already she was off down the track. 'See you at the house,' she called, raising an arm but not looking back.

I made certain the tailgate was secure, then walked across to the nearest fir. There was no rush. Watering the tree I thought contentedly of Hinnawi's new shipment. Any day now it would dock and the funds would be transferred. Another satisfactory conclusion. The Gulf continued to hold the best promise. As long as oil or religion remained, its greedy little squabbles would need to be furnished. I returned to the car and sat there, eyes closed, letting the fan cool my face.

So here you are at last, I reflected. In the Montazeau woodyard. Where things are sawn down and other things mended. All very apt. But your judgement was wanting — that's what should trouble you. The demarcation, public and private, always used to be absolute. Before her, you let no one across. Take it as a warning.

I open my eyes. It's time. There'll be questions of course, procedure, but nothing of consequence. Accidents occur, without reason or purpose. Most simply confirm our fragility; the daily, unconscious dance between breath and oblivion.

Happily my calculation is sound. I spot her first at some distance through the trees, above me as she climbs. Yellow blouse like a target. I see her long back curving forward, the way she's raised in the pedals, grinding slowly uphill. Foolish girl. Despite the exertion, the wet cotton glued to her already, I can picture her smiling with pleasure.

I have to smile too, glancing down at the bouldered ravine. Wherever you are, cycling just isn't safe. Rounding another hairpin, she comes into view.

I change down and accelerate.

The Never-Still and the Stars

SUHARI ROLLED OVER. For one blissful moment he had no sensation at all. Then he felt the hard earth beneath him and groaned. He was awake.

Without opening his eyes he knew it was soon after four: the first *becaks* were astir, creaking by on the bridge above. Motionless, he lay listening to the plink of their bells. The smell of browning chicken reached him with the woodsmoke of fires already lit across the river. Hunger grumbled inside him. With concentration he began to breathe through his mouth and after a while the longing receded. Only now, stretching out on the mat with his hands behind his head, did he open his eyes.

Above were the stars. *Darkness is a friend*, he thought, *and now it is going*. He repeated the phrase, half-aloud, gazing upward. Slowly he realised he had woken from a dream and was seeing and speaking what he had dreamt. *Night is the cloak of all beggars*. Again he spoke the words softly. They escaped on his breath without thought. He had not an instant's doubt Who was responsible. Only his own certainty frightened him. *Kehendak Tuhan berlaku,* he said. God wills it. He knew now why the night was important. His dream lay before him with the clarity of the stars . . .

Inclining his head, he saw that his mother and the

child, even his father, had yet to stir. Without a sound he sat up, pulled on his shorts and went quietly across to the fire. Yesterday's embers still smouldered. He set some sticks on the coals, hunkered down and blew softly till they caught. Then he took the old oil drum, the fold of wire-mesh, and edged down the bank. The dust softened to mud, was warm between his toes. He waded out a few steps till water lapped at his waist. Here the current and air moved a little. Holding the filter over the drum, he pushed it under, a tiny brown whirlpool; returned the slopping container to the bank. Nearby he crouched in the shallows, relieved and washed himself, clambered out. The fire crackled warmly now beneath the improvised trivet. Later, Ibu would reboil the water so the baby could drink. She had no milk left of her own.

Suhari dried his feet by the flames. Once he had tied his shoes (a pair of mouldering trainers several sizes too large, retrieved by his father only last week from the dump) he sat still for a minute, looking back at the stars. His gaze ranged slowly from one cluster to the next. By now they were quite familiar to him, these shapes the brightest ones made when he joined them together. To each he had given a name (Krisno, Susu, Rama . . .), whatever had suggested itself when first he saw it. When the early sky was clear, his most pressing need was to identify each friend before he rose, before they vanished. He often got up believing he would not see them again; but he told no one of this. His mother was preoccupied with the baby. He realized it was important to her that Sita should live, but in eight months he doubted she had heard anything he said. As for his father, Suhari knew he would merely be angry, say what he always said now: 'Boys of seven should outgrow such nonsense . . .' Even with Bang, his closest friend, he dared not speak of it. Bang had the habit of laughing at everything.

Double-checking his pocket — the coins his father had given him last night — he ducked through the railings and made his way up to the bridge. Across the road, Bang was already waiting, his peak-capped silhouette against a pale bar of sky. Suhari dodged between the early cars — spluttering forward like monstrous beetles — and touched his friend on the shoulder.

'*Hai, kamu!*'

For a moment, before the usual wide smile returned, Suhari was shocked at how serious Bang looked as he swung around. He'd never seen this expression before and it frightened him. But once the grin was there again and Bang had put an arm round his shoulder and they'd started to walk, Hari wondered if he might not have imagined it — those stern eyes staring right through him.

From some invisible mosque along the river, the amplified voice of the *adhan* began to tell of God's greatness. It was the hour of prayer.

'*Jum'at*,' muttered Suhari. The Holy Day. They were approaching Seno's shop; along the road he made out the old man's bent figure, setting up his stall.

'Don't worry, I haven't forgotten,' Bang responded. His gawky arms swung as he walked. 'But later, OK? We can pray before noon, at *Adhan lohor*.'

Deep down, Suhari disapproved of his friend's laxity where their faith was concerned. Yet Bang had always protected him so in general he bit his tongue; rarely showed how he felt when Bang called him *adik*, 'little brother,' or argued that prayer never changed things. But now he had his own plans.

'No,' he replied evenly, 'it must wait till tonight, till

Adhan ashar. Today I'm not stopping till I have three thousand.'

'*Demi Allah!* Are you mad? You've got the fever again.' Bang laid a palm on his forehead. 'It would take us three days—three *good* days—to make that! Do you hear what he's saying, Bapa?'

They had reached the shop. Bang turned to Seno, the old Sundanese, then back to Suhari, grinning in disbelief. 'Three *thousand*? Selling gum—at five rupes a time? A pair of ruffians like us?'

Seno chuckled. 'No need to dodge cars if you can manage that. Why not buy my whole stock!' He went on counting out their supply of sweets and matches.

Hari frowned at them both. Why did no one ever listen? 'No, Bang,' he said. 'Not two of us. Each. I mean three thousand *each*.'

At least this time Bang didn't laugh. He opened his mouth to say something but then simply shrugged and smiled. In a way Hari felt disappointed not to be pressed further. Bang and Seno shared the fault of most older people: they assumed that whatever he said had no basis in reason. He passed the old man his coins, a hundred *rupiah*. So did Bang. To the elder boy Seno handed six boxes of Lucky Strike matches; to Suhari, ten slim packs of chewing gum.

'Good luck, *gelandangan*,' he said.

Hearing this, Suhari felt a small charge of pride. The elation would dissapate quickly enough in the heat of the morning, one driver after another shaking his head, waving dismissal from the air-conditioned cool. By then dodging traffic with a trayful of gum would seem what it was: demeaning, perilous, absurd: something only the desperate would contemplate. But whatever grand offices and sparkling hotels the occupants of taxis and limousines had access to, here was one club — The Never-Still, the streets' numberless army — they could never belong to . . .

Suhari looked up at his friend as they moved into Wahid Hasyim. The jauntiness of the baseball cap, its long peak tilted back, made him smile with affection. Once again he wished Bang was his real brother, and (for the hundredth time) set about trying to copy his loose-limbed swaggery walk.

Just this side of Jalan Thamrin, the six-lane highway where most of their day would be spent, lamps and car-bide-flares glowed among the backstreet *warungs*, the semi-permanent eating stalls. Boys fanned at flames with banana leaves. Smoke hung in veils. Gesturing diners were cast onto canvas and walls in spidery outlines — living echoes of the stylised shadow-plays, the hundred demons ranged against Krisno and his followers. Here and there along the roadside, the *pikulunan* — sinewy, steel-wire men (heads thrust forward, backs bent beneath the pressure of their bowing shoulder-poles) were setting down boxes and baskets to reveal soups, noodles, sweetmeats.

Bang led Suhari to a nearby *kaki lima* — or 'five-legged man' — whose kitchen, a hybrid of bicycle and counter, was secured near the kerb on a tripod of props.

Klok . . . klok . . . klok . . . The familiar hollow echo — ox-horn tapped with a stick — announced that his stall today offered *bakso*, a nourishing meatball gruel. *Klok . . . klok . . . klok . . .* Suhari found himself shivering as they drew nearer. Today this most ordinary of sounds unsettled him, he couldn't say why. The stallholder, his face half-obscured beneath the bamboo hat, tapped out the signal like a wizened *gamelan* musician.

Suhari watched as the *bakso*-man spooned out two bowls. From under the brim of the *topi* (a country hat, strangely out of place here) the man's breath came in gasps and hisses. *Herrr. . .Herrr. . .Ayyy*. Was he speaking? To himself? To them? As soon as his bowl was ready Suhari grabbed it, squatted down by the wall next to Bang.

'Why here?' he asked quietly. They were still within earshot.

'Why not?' grinned Bang. He held the bowl under his chin, ladling in soft balls of meat.

'We eat at Chaiyo's.'

'It's not the law.' Bang began to look irritated. 'Why? Gone off *bakso* all of a sudden?'

'It's OK.' Suhari stole a glance over his shoulder. The old man looked quickly away to the person he was serving, but not quickly enough. It was clear he'd been watching him. '*Cap cai*'s better, though.' Suhari turned back to Bang. 'And cheaper. I feel bad wasting Ayah's money . . .'

'Oh, come on. You're always guilty at something. You'll feel worse if you don't eat. He can't expect you to work on thin air. Not *every* day.'

'Well, it's disloyal to Chaiyo. He'll wonder where we are.'

Bang lowered his bowl, wiped grease from his mouth with the back of his hand. 'You're my friend, Hari,' he sighed, 'but sometimes I wish you weren't. I don't need a good conscience, do I? I've got you.'

Suhari smiled feebly. He hated himself sometimes. The way he came out with things, whatever entered his head. He didn't want to be good. Being good just annoyed people, made them mistrust you. Nobody survived in this city by doing the right thing or observing the law. And why should they, when nobody did right by them? But still. It was as if something, some*body*, inside him was there to step in and prevent it, the moment he threatened to behave like everyone else. Bang was right. Other people were different. And one day, maybe today, Bang would get up and leave him, he knew. Would finally have enough of his stupid piety. Suhari couldn't blame him, but was powerless to stop it.

'Finished?,' Bang asked.

He nodded a reply. Tipped up the bowl and licked out the last bit of juice. 'Are we going to see Chaiyo now?'

The strange mournful tokking of the *kerbau*-horn had resumed. Suhari was on his feet quickly, glad to leave. As they did so he turned and looked at the man; again felt himself tremble. He saw Bang hesitate too — with the same deep frown he'd seen earlier on the bridge — then move quickly away.

'It's you who's after this miracle,' Bang said. 'So tell me . . . have we time for social calls?'

'He's our *friend*. He'll wonder where we are. What's eating you, anyway?'

Kicking a can to the gutter, Bang muttered something.

'I don't like you like this.' Hari thrust a hand grumpily down the front of his shorts and scratched himself. 'You scare me.'

They'd come to another crossing in the warren of side streets. This whole area was known as Kebon Kacang, the Bean Garden. It might have been once, though Suhari couldn't picture it. All around them was concrete. Hidden at the back of the smart big road, no beans were growing here now, not even in the mud-yellow pools where the surface had buckled.

'This was going to be a special day,' he added quietly. Now all he had was a sense of foreboding. That something was changing, but not as he planned.

A half-empty *bemo* whined by next to the pavement. The ticket-boy leaned out calling *teng . . . teng . . . teng . . . teng* very fast. He raised his slim eyebrows into question-marks and pointed. Bang shook his head and the vehicle growled on. A little enviously, Suhari continued to watch the slim figure hanging languidly out, slipstream ruffling his hair. The bell-like refrain grew fainter, swallowed up by the city awakening.

'*Ma'af, dik.*' Bang rested a hand lightly on his shoulder. 'I'm sorry. It's not your fault.'

They crossed over. In the time it took to reach the far side, Bang's mood appeared to have brightened. 'You're right, we'll do well today,' he smiled cheerfully. 'I feel it. Come on . . . a few minutes with Chaiyo then. It's still early.'

He meant too early for rush hour. Before the real jams started they'd be wasting their time. Luckily, that wasn't often. Built by Sukarno as a showcase highway, back in the days when his city still fought for world recognition, the 'golden mile' of Thamrin still created the required illusion for those who stood at the hotel- and embassy-windows lining its route. Directly beneath them, all was apparent speed and efficiency. (So Bang had explained it to him). But once out of their sight, what happened to the traffic or the roads or the people who used them was of no concern to the government. From the Presidential Palace and Merdeka Field to the north, past the Hotels Indonesia and Mandarin, right down to where Police Headquarters stood, so reassuringly, opposite the gates of the Hilton — at its heart the new capital was a lie, an assembly of mirrors. Like the gold-tipped monument ('Sukarno's tool,' ran the oldest joke of all) this part of their city was no more within reach of most citizens than the shelves of the Merlin Department Store. Perhaps only scavengers like Bang and himself looked upon the area, with its towering steel backdrops, as in any way their home. For at both ends of Thamrin were the junctions where, each day at first light, they and countless others made ready. Where cars were soon logjammed, fuming in the smog, hour upon hour. Trapped and resigned, besieged by paperboys, cigarette-touts, ice-sellers—most drivers gave in eventually. Rolled down a window and bought.

Nonetheless, competition was cut-throat, sometimes literally. All around the prized intersections ran invisible boundaries. One might share rice and a joke at the *warung*, but once business began it was wise to forget about friendship. Just a few weeks ago Hari had witnessed a knife-fight among the Mercedes, eight in the morning, whole gangs leaping the bonnets like stepping-stones. For several nights afterward he'd sat up sweating, the scene still wet in his mind. Red droplets like rain on the windshield, the limp shape slipping down as the sirens began . . .

Maybe Bang was recalling this too as they reached Chaiyo's alley. There was urgency in his walk despite what he'd said, and Suhari struggled to keep up. Today, with his madcap plan, there was only one place—the circular island at the end of Kebon Kacang, the busiest area, where Sultan Syarir and Imam Bonjol converged. Drivers, *gelandangan*, police: everyone functioned on edge here.

They talked briefly with Chaiyo. He gave them some tea, extra sugar. Even Suhari, who adored anything sweet, couldn't help wincing.

'*Tch.* You two.' Chaiyo's tongue clicked. 'Take all the energy you can get.'

Suhari knocked back the glass in one gulp, holding his breath. *Paman* Chaiyo wouldn't be the same without his gruffness, his bullying advice. Quite how he had adopted them, or they him, it was hard to remember. Still, it was a fact of life—one of few he felt certain of, held firm to. Until this morning he hadn't doubted that Bang felt the same way. But the way his friend had led him to the

unknown *bakso*-man, breaking their routine, continued to
trouble Suhari. And whereas Bang's usual style was to pull
Chaiyo's leg, mimic his seriousness with affection, when
Suhari looked across now to account for his silence, he
saw a face more morose than any the old man had shown
them. Seated on a packing case, Bang stared down emptily
at his glass, the ridges of his shoulder blades sharp beneath
his T-shirt.

'What's the matter?' hissed Suhari. A woman had come
up to Chaiyo and was asking the way.

'It's nothing.' Bang didn't look up.

'Come on. Between you and Chaiyo. Since yesterday.'

Bang toyed with the glass, shook his head. 'It's not the
old man. Not really.'

'He's been good to us. Like an uncle. We've always
shown him an uncle's respect. Now today you don't even
look at him. And you say nothing's wrong?'

Bang stood up suddenly. 'Later,' he said tersely,
bending close to Suhari and taking his glass. 'I'll tell you
later. That's a promise.' He returned the glasses to Chaiyo
with a little bow. 'Now come on — or forget all your
dreams . . .'

Some time ago Suhari remembered his father saying he
would soon have a brother or sister to play with. But
he'd heard that before, and nothing had come of it. He'd
felt no great pleasure or surprise, wondering only why
his father wasn't more clear. A boy or a girl — didn't he
know? Mystified, Suhari had returned to his task: cutting
open cigarette stubs, one by one, tipping the few threads
of unsmoked tobacco and *cengkih* into a small hemp sack.
(They had many other sacks — full of odds and ends

garnered from refuse tips, street cans, unattended trucks — but this was the one they guarded most carefully, which hung on its own special hook beneath the bridge. If their own shelter of sacks blew down in a storm, if a cloudburst reduced them to dripping rags, that was one thing. But for a five kilo sack of *tembakau* to suffer the same fate — a single one could take two months to fill — that would be too much to bear). By the following evening, when his father returned with two thousand *rupiah* from the sale of the sack, Suhari had forgotten all about babies.

Personally he'd no wish to share Ibu and Ayah with anyone — especially brothers or sisters. One was more than enough. But luckily, though his parents kept searching, it was clear they weren't looking in the right place. Suhari smiled. Allah listened to his prayers. And, sure enough, this time too the pattern was repeated. His father took him aside while Ibu was resting. (Hari had heard her cry out the night before — her bad dreams repeating, he assumed. Rolled over and gone back to sleep). Next day his father had an arm round his shoulder, pretending not to weep. They'd lost another, he said. Hari nodded, frowning. Told him not to cry. But inside he was wondering, after such a long search, how they could be so careless. Why he'd never seen the earlier ones either, before they too were lost.

He was past the threshold of exhaustion, too excited to sleep. Still, he lay down. The stars were in their place. And the wad of rolled notes, close to his three thousand target, glowed in his pocket.

For almost twelve hours he'd made light of the heat,

threats from drivers and rivals, their wild-eyed obscenities. Five or six times he'd sprinted back and forth from the highway to Seno, gathered up fresh supplies. The old man was speechless; Suhari inspired. Not till well after dark had he and Bang left the highway, made their slow way home, aching and laughing, drawing out the day as long as they could. A day, Suhari sensed, when he'd crossed some new threshold; where he and Bang, the bond between them that earlier had seemed under threat, had reached a new place. Their difference in age had somehow eroded. Perhaps, he thought happily, I am no longer young.

He looked across at his father and mother, making ready for the night. He'd sworn Bang to secrecy. Maybe tomorrow he'd feel different, would tell Bu and Ayah. Then again, he could always find a safe hiding place, somewhere no one but he would know of it. Put some aside, day by day. Anything was possible now.

Suhari. 'Good Eye', his name meant. Because of this he believed he was born lucky. One day people would sit up and take notice, his name would be known. Then he would buy Uncle Yeddi, the *becak* driver, the Honda taxi he'd spent a lifetime talking about; and Sri, his aunt, could be done with the idiot's cursing. And, of course, he'd set up his parents, little sister, in the best house on Jalan Sitibundo: one with big gates, shady trees . . .

The vividness of his dream came back to him. Each minute in the streets, along the shacks of the canals, someone died and was buried in their threadbare *kain*, their worm-eaten shirt. But nobody could be presented to Allah like this. So all across the sky the Prophets were busy, washing the poor (so numerous that sometimes the springs of heaven overflowed, drowning the earth) before dressing them anew in spotless white garments. Not a thread of cloth would be wasted though — every tatter laid carefully aside. It was these, at God's command, that the angels had used since the beginning of time to patch the night's cloak. Without pause they stitched and sewed on, striving to mend each hole and tear, but even this proved beyond them. When first they explained this to God, He had smiled. Yes, He told them, it is as it should be. This way a little of heaven would always be visible from earth: man, woman or child—none should feel excluded from His light. And the hungry and the sick—they could simply look up and know their importance to God. For He had used their own rags to shelter the world.

Turning this in his mind, Suhari decided that only the rich feared the dark. The rest surely thought as he—that only the promise of night made each day bearable. These beautiful hours, beneath a blanket of stars or the hammer of rain, when one could plummet into sleep and forget.

True North

THE CAB BRINGS me straight from her apartment but it's later than I'd planned. For early October it's bitter, cold enough to snow, and the light's already fading.

Entering the gates I clutch the flowers in both hands—a beacon of red, white and blue on this dull afternoon—and try to hurry down the half-frozen path without slipping. I'd hoped to fulfil her wishes with dignity, but now I feel flustered again, unbalanced, shuffling forward like a novice skater. Like a fool I left the walking-stick behind—more from pride than forgetfulness. When a woman seeks your help due to infirmity, entrusts you with a mission this close to her heart, you want to appear at least mobile yourself.

If there's one place to remind you of frailty however, it's here. In the thirty-odd years since Glenn's funeral I've scarcely been back. Only for Jeanie's, and her plot (ours, I should say) is some distance off, a quite different section. These are older, swankier grounds and the trees appear taller and denser, the graves less tightly packed. *Straight ahead from the gate, parallel with Mt. Pleasant Avenue . . .* Just as well the old lady gave me directions for I recognise little.

Then all of a sudden I see it. The family memorial, raised on its plinth. A few steps away, laid flat in the turf,

Glenn's simple marker. A piano's outline, the opening bars of the Goldberg, inscribed on the marble.

Bending stiffly I place the bouquet beside it on the near-frozen grass. The care and love in her choice is evident. A spray of belladonna delphiniums, asiatic lilies. Snapdragons, gladioli too, set off by slender green stems. A sunburst of colour against the grey stone, the thickening dusk.

My knees object as I straighten, sciatica jabs at the pit of my back. A little cloud forms with each gasp. The light will be gone soon and the taxi's there waiting. Snug in the depths of my greatcoat I locate the flask. Two quick nips and the whiskey spreads through my chest, a pleasing whoosh of fire. Replacing the cap I delve again for the envelope, a nervous reflex, just to be sure it's still there.

It is, flat against my breast in the inside pocket. But now the time's come to honour her other request, I realise I need a few moments. Though their story's a matter of record, I still find it hard to take in. For how many years did I witness Glenn shrinking from intimacy? Hypersensitive, neurotic, obsessed with germs and avoiding them, the prospect of a handshake filled him with terror, never mind a kiss . . .

Images, memories of Glenn — boy and man — flash before me. Snatches of his voice — that tumbling, excitable torrent. Looks — challenging, appreciative, dismissive. I thought that age might have cured me of sentiment but perhaps I was wrong. It feels good to be close to him again, at least in spirit.

There's a bench a few paces off but I need to keep moving. My fingers and feet are already numb. I set off again cautiously. There's more grip just off the path, where the grass is beginning to frost. One small circuit through the trees for my own small . . .

I was going to say *prayer*. But in truth I've not prayed in a long time, feel largely a sham when I try. No, just time to reflect. And it has to be now, I know that. Next time I'm here—west quadrant, plot 701, tucked up with Jeanie—I can leave the reflecting to others.

I can guess what they'll say though: *Much loved this . . .distinguished the other . . .* And what most will be thinking: *What a fool. What a pompous, deluded old fool.*

In many ways we were always those boys.

I see him quite clearly, edging into that schoolroom, our first morning at Williamson Road. Frowning, taking all of us in with studied concentration. A dark-haired, slightly-built kid—seven years old like the rest of us, just as anxious of what lay ahead. I noticed his ears, I remember: small, rather prominent ears. How he seemed to be mumbling, maybe humming to himself as he searched for a seat.

This must be sixty . . . no, more than seventy years ago. (Is it *possible?*) He sits down at the desk next to mine. Gives me that shy half-smile I came to know well. I ask him his name, tell him mine, then we just sit there awaiting the teacher, staring anxiously out at that huge grey yard, the leaves swirling across it.

Later they sent us all out there, the whole lower school. Kicking balls, throwing them, running and screaming. After a while I must have sensed Glenn's absence. Looked around and spotted him, way off by the fence, prancing alone in light-footed circles, waving his arms as he went. I know I was bewildered, transfixed. Had seen nothing like it, for sure—that strange, balletic dance. And once I drew closer I could hear he was singing—singing in an unknown language as he glided around me. Eyelids fluttering, almost closed, face lit from within by that half-detached smile. I can only describe it as some form of trance, one he was utterly lost to . . .

Until, that is, a group of older, much bigger, kids were suddenly swarming about us—poking and shoving and taunting him.

Little ballerina . . . look how pretty he is . . . he must be a girl . . . let's take a look . . .

For sure, I'm no hero, then or since, and I'm certain it made little difference, whatever it was that I said. The idiots may have paused for a second, told me to mind my own business, but I know Glenn crept home that first day with some fierce aches and bruises. Whatever footling intervention I'd made though, he clearly felt it enough to consider me an ally, one of the few in a place he soon loathed. The next day we did speak a little, discovered we were practically neighbours across Southwood Avenue. Invited into his house I heard those strange words again, discovered they were German, something called *lieder*. I'd no idea what that meant but sat there amazed as Glenn's spider-like fingers floated over the keys, raising exquisite sounds as his mother sang. Later, over tea, he introduced me to his goldfish—Beethoven, Haydn, Chopin and Bach—along with a tiny pale bird he called Mozart. He also kept rabbits outside, even a turtle and skunk. Above all there was Nick—a huge Irish setter who followed him everywhere. It was the first glimpse I had of Glenn's lifelong devotion to animals. I could see he found them much easier than people. But that was the start of our friendship, I guess: our shared love of music . . .

Another nip from the flask. The irony is, Glenn would have loved it here. The cold and the quiet; this bleached-out, black-and-white scene. Despite his paranoia about 'catching a chill' (from which he'd project all manner of obscure but life-threatening outcomes) Glenn much preferred winter to any other season. From our earliest days he'd shrink from strong sunlight, bright colours too—be it toys, book covers, clothing. And the older he got—the more he grew wary of people and crowds and performing in public—this kind of solitude was just what he craved.

The three or four boys who'd tormented him wouldn't let it lie. A week or two later they cornered us somewhere inside and I feared for us both, Glenn's hands in particular. We'd learned quickly enough that these were what made him special, how fearful he was of their damage. I never saw him pick up a ball, never mind catch or throw one. It was rumoured that Florrie, his mother, as unbending a force as Dr Kirkpatrick, our fearsome Principal, had extracted a promise that her son be exempted from all forms of sport or potential physical contact. Which, of course, only made his status as *sissy* and *mummy's boy*, as the 'genius freak', still more assured. It wasn't his only dispensation. *Run home to mama* the same morons hissed when Glenn would leave early for more practice or lessons.

But what none of us had seen till that day was the other side of Glenn. One you crossed at your peril. It shocked the hell out of them, and of me. He moved toward them with such purpose, such a murderous look in his eye, that the whole gang took a step back. In that single moment, before Glenn even spoke, the whole dynamic had changed. He closed in on their leader, a big blond boy, till they were just inches apart.

'If you ever come near me again I shall kill you. Are we clear?' Staring him down.

The boy tried to laugh but you could see he was no longer sure. Like the rest of us he must've been thinking:

this kid is different, he's strange, you can't predict what he'll do, what he's capable of. When Glenn went to push his way by, their ranks simply parted and I followed him out.

In years to come I'd have to endure this same force of will, a fierce single-mindedness that swept opposition aside. But this was the first mini–crisis we shared and our lives were intertwined from here on.

And that was the last time at school I saw anyone bother him.

I think he found it preposterous, a form of betrayal perhaps, that four decades later I was back at Williamson, this time as Principal, one of Kirkpatrick's successors. But the place was in my blood, on the whole I'd been happy there—in part because I knew Glenn. And forty-odd years had brought many improvements, most for the best, a trend I hoped to continue.

I was forty-seven by then, Jeanie almost ten years younger. We'd just had our twelfth anniversary. That would make Harriet ten, Tim just shy of eight, when they started at Williamson too. I'd worked my way up the ranks at the Dundas and Huron Street Junior Schools, but this was the job I had coveted and by the time it fell vacant my case was well-founded. We moved to a house we all loved on Bellefair Avenue, where the kids grew and prospered; the home I still rattle around in, just a stone's-throw from Southwood where Glenn and I were raised.

Naturally I'd followed each step of his comet-like rise. Had barely started as a teacher at Dundas when the Goldberg LP, his signature work, was released. From nowhere to stardom, as if overnight. I pored over every review, trailed Jeanie from room to room, reading her the latest, punching the air at each new garland. Back then we were both in a state of euphoria. Still deeply in love, aware of the luck in our lives, thrilled at a friend's success. A million years from mortality.

Our library of Glenn recordings grew along with us. When time and chance allowed I attended his concerts — from the first time he tried out the Goldberg here in Toronto (to an all-but-empty hall, assailed by Hurricane Hazel) to a dazzling night in New York (a regular stop-off to see Jeanie's parents) where Glenn's rendition of Bach fugues, the Brahms Quintet for Piano and Strings — his mesmerizing blend of melancholy and elation — truly moved us to tears.

I'd played the violin myself since 2nd Grade, inspired and intimidated by my closest friend's talent, and as the years passed did my utmost to keep up my playing. By nineteen I'd switched to viola, preferring its richer, full-bodied voice; was trying out in various quartets and small chamber groups. My first and last solo performance came at a young cousin's wedding — the off-notes, to my ear, amplified cruelly in the echoey church — an experience too unnerving to repeat. Without doubt though, my most treasured recollections are of laughter-filled, informal evenings, dueting with Glenn. After dinner at our house or a mutual friend's. Up at his family cottage in Orillia, a space for privacy and reflection that he'd jealously guarded. Beside Bert and Florrie, his parents, only those he most trusted were ever allowed there. Playing quietly beside him, a musical genius — just the two of us in that magical setting — I felt doubly honoured. United in and through the music, we rarely felt closer.

All the same, I learned early that fallouts with Glenn were inevitable. It was simply how he was. The closer he allowed you to get (and this was something he granted to few) the more vulnerable, edgy and resistant he became.

In any case, whatever the reason, it was soon after I took up the Williamson reins that my last rift with Glenn became apparent. I hoped he'd be pleased for me, but not for the first time he simply stopped calling. Then failed to respond to my letters or calls. Friendship, music, his schedule — it was always life on his terms. We'd been here before and I knew all the signs. He'd take umbrage, cut ties abruptly — at the slightest cause. A misconstrued look, wholly innocent remark.

The first serious occasion it happened I recall very clearly — some fifteen years earlier in Chicago, almost his final concert appearance. (Was he 30? 32? God, what a waste!) Jeanie and I hadn't long met. Naturally she'd heard from me all about Glenn but this was her first chance to hear him play live — and to meet him. Shown backstage to his dressing-room afterwards, we found Glenn casting aside the suit and sharp shoes he'd performed in, wrapping himself back into sweaters and gloves, his beloved flat cap and boots. As ever he complained of shoulder pains, a cold; never stopped checking that the heating was going full blast. (Not long before this — someplace in Florida I think — he'd been detained in some park as a vagrant; a not unreasonable assumption given this penchant for well-worn all-weather clothing, even at 90°. It probably hadn't helped that he claimed to be a world–famous pianist, appearing that night at the Symphony Hall).

As the rest of us strove not to faint in that dressing-room he looked haggard and pale, more than usually fretful about how the evening had gone.

'I can't do it anymore. I messed it up totally. You can't fail to have noticed . . .'

He couldn't keep still, pacing from mirror to basin, rolling up his sleeves, dipping his arms in hot water.

'My shoulders, this arm—they just froze. I heard the whole theatre gasp. Well, lucky them—they got what they came for, as ever. Not the music of course, just a damned spectacle. Someone to gawp at, pull apart . . .'

I couldn't help thinking back to the schoolyard. He'd not lost the feeling that the world was against him; that human nature, in essence, was wickedly cruel.

'They must've left the place laughing. *Did you see him? He's lost it, he's washed up for sure* . . . Well, maybe I am. In any case, this is it—finito. No more concerts or tours, no more performing seal . . .'

Then he just sat there, head in his hands, but when he looked up at me all the fire and the anger had gone and I recognised that look. The scared, cornered kid.

'Come on—be honest, Paul. Was it so bad? How did I do?'

I remember hesitating, conscious of Glenn's sensitivity. I was also aware how closely aligned he held friendship and honesty.

'The Partita was glorious, and the Krenek. The Beethoven, well . . . I daresay there were moments . . .'

Glenn's take on the late sonatas, though original, was wildly at odds with Beethoven's written instructions, in particular with regard to tempo changes in the different movements. Glenn thrived and insisted on this, of course; was dismissive of the concert-goer's preference for tradition. So I felt on safeish ground here, limiting reservations to something he already knew.

'The first movement was quite pacey . . . *allegro con brio* outdid the *appassionata* . . .'

Even so, I reminded him, the audience had stood and applauded for close to five minutes—and that was *after* he departed the stage. They'd come away thrilled, as had we. Yet in that one, two sentences of faintest concurrence with those he saw as detractors, the ignorant crowd, I saw his look change and withdraw. He mumbled it was good to meet Jeanie then turned away to talk to his manager.

A month later, true to his word, he gave his last public recital in Los Angeles. I didn't hear from him again in nearly a year. At the time, as Jeanie will attest, I was crest-fallen, almost in mourning. Thought our friendship was ruined for good, over nothing. Then early one evening I opened our door and there he stood, beaming, shoving roses into my hand saying 'These are for Jeanie,' striding past me into the hall. He stayed for dinner, played a hilarious duet with me and talked about his upcoming schedule as if we'd been together all year. Intolerable, infuriating, childlike Glenn. By the end of the night it seemed churlish, nay impossible, not to forgive him.

Some years later I incurred similar displeasure for suggesting to a clearly overweight, heavily perspiring travesty of Glenn—one I barely recognised—that the pills he was downing to stop his hands shaking, to get him to sleep, to counter his lethargy, the spasms in his shoulders and back—that in all probability these were as much cause as the cure. Same result. No contact for months. Then suddenly he'd be there again, bursting back into our lives like a meteor, as only he could.

And I always let it slide. This was Glenn, after all, and I'd seen the whole story. From the start he'd brought the mysterious and unpredictable into my life, and whenever this vanished I missed him terribly.

But little by little I could sense Jeanie's patience wear thin, see her forced smile in his presence, feel her whole being tighten when his name came up.

❧

Night-owl that he was, when the phone rang at two or three in the morning, as it often did through the early years of our marriage, we both knew it was Glenn. (These days it's more likely to be Harriet, warring with Rick, who's stormed out again; or Tim juiced up in some bar, trying to figure how his latest band died).

The last time Glenn called me like this was in the Fall of '82. We'd not long re-established a truce on my Williamson status. Without explicit discussion, we each knew not to speak of it. My head rose from the pillow still foggy with dreams and fatigue. It was pitch-dark outside, just hours before I was due at the airport. Denver, our annual headteacher's conference. Not that Glenn would care, never mind ask. He'd be so engrossed—cocooned in the cave of his St Clair apartment, writing, reading, composing—that the hours others keep would mean nothing.

'Listen, Paul. I've had the most wonderful gift. Glorious. Transcendent. You simply must hear it.'

I'd heard on the grapevine he hadn't been well—hypertension, gout, genuine and serious infections this time. But now he sounded upbeat, inspired, full of his old manic energy.

'Well, that's great, Glenn. Of course. And we've missed you . . .'

But he was on his own path.

'Never mind that, not now. We'll catch up, but first you must hear it.'

His excitement was audible down the line. Since turning his back on the stage Glenn had retreated to the studio—pushing on with a punishing schedule of recordings and, increasingly, scripting and producing documentaries for TV and radio. Memorable, bewildering, provocative in equal measure—pure Glenn, in fact—it was largely through these I'd kept track of his progress through 'the absent times'. With his memorable *Solitude Trilogy* still fresh in my head, I assumed his latest inspiration concerned a new broadcasting project. From boyhood I'd been keenly aware of his desire to write, to create and compose. Performance and performers to him were ephemeral, soon forgotten. No, it was creators whom people remembered and Glenn made no secret that he craved this kind of legacy.

The idea of 'north,' even the word, had obsessed him for as long as I knew. Way before he visited those vast, barely habited places they seemed to hold for him all the positives he longed for. Solitude. Freedom. Escape from the crowds, from expectations heaped upon him since his fingers first touched the keys.

'If there's a truth,' he'd say, 'it's not here. Here is just noise and distraction. Somewhere else is the heartbeat of everything, Paul. We just have to listen. Wind and rain, birdsong, every animal voice. It's all that I need. All any of us need . . .'

Even when we were kids he'd talk all the time of the Northern Territories, its rivers and mountains, how forests and fields run for ever up there. How one day he'd just leave, head up there alone, build his own cabin and never come back.

'Right out in the wilderness, Paul, just me and the animals. Sick and stray dogs, old cattle and horses. Space for us all to be happy, to live out our days . . .'

And years later he'd add: 'Where's there no chance I'll bump into a critic.'

It was an enviable vision. To live as one wished, openly, without hindrance. I was hypnotised by how he'd describe it. Glenn and versions of Glenn have appeared in my dreams ever since—always some mythic adventurer, trudging on through forests and snowscapes. For me, once awake, that other world melts quickly away, but Glenn held on to it right to the end, an almost childlike belief that all things were possible.

And he did make some short trips up there — to Manitoulin and Churchill, Coral Harbor, Hudson Bay. Tape-recording ordinary people, their voices and wilderness sounds; splicing them together in counterpoint back in the studio. It gave him a taste of the dream, though never the total withdrawal he longed for.

'No, no,' he rushed on down the phone, impatient at my semi-comatose response. 'It's music, Paul — music! A fugue. I'm composing again! I have it all down. Celestial, I'm telling you. It was there in my sleep, the whole thing, I just woke and transcribed it, the last couple of nights. You'll be the first, the very first to hear it. Honestly, it's perfect, it'll blow you away. My legacy, Paul. C'mon, drive over now . . . I'll set you up a martini and play it straight through. What you say? Be worth it, I promise.'

I didn't doubt that it would. Despite the hour and my imminent schedule, the prospect of a new composition, being forever the first to experience it, all but persuaded me.

'Glenn, I'd love to, you know that. But right now it's impossible . . .'

'C'mon, Paul . . .'

I filled him in on Colorado. 'I'll be back next week though. How about one evening then? I'm dying to hear it . . .'

To my eternal regret, once I got home I had much to catch up on, plunged back into school and governor business. It was ever so. Glenn was still on my call-list when the news broke. The massive stroke he had suffered, the coma. Within days he was gone.

Since then, whenever I imagine his spirit, it's up there in the north.

❧

For the last six years of her life, once our former guest-room held my permanent bed, Jeanie wasn't disturbed any more by these early-hours calls, no longer had to hear me utter Glenn's name. Not since that night when the years of frustration burst from her like a volcano. It still brings me out in a sweat when I think of it. The night that changed us for good.

Jeanie and I at that time were making one final effort to rescue our marriage, the intimacy we'd somehow misplaced long before. We went out to dinner again, the theatre; sought to rekindle the days of our courtship. We'd never really argued up to this point, simply grown older, over-comfortable. We knew one another so well that surprise seemed impossible, we'd run out of new things to say. I suppose it's called drifting apart.

It's true that much of the impetus to change this, to turn back the clock, did come from her. And though I still loved and admired her for trying, I grew more and more distracted, resigned, as my body failed to respond.

But when the phone rang that night — rolling away from her as gently as I could: *please, Jeanie, no. I just can't* — I was quite unprepared for what followed.

'Oh yes . . . go on. We know who *that* is. He calls and you jump, nothing changes there. Christ, it's *him* you should have married! Would have saved us half-a-lifetime of this . . . this *obsession!*'

She sat up sharply, pulled the covers up around her. ' "Glenn this, Glenn that . . ." ' — I've smiled, held my tongue, put up with it for God knows how long. But *not* any more. Don't mention him again in my hearing, not ever! Understand? And when you've taken that call, you can sleep somewhere else. I don't want you anywhere near me . . .'

It was a brutal shock to us both. From the moment I withdrew down the landing I began to reassess everything. As far as I knew I loved Jeanie as dearly as ever, had always believed that she knew it. Until her outburst I'd felt just as secure in her love for me. But as she'd made clear, I'd been blind and complacent, taken so much for granted.

The kids, of course, soon picked up on all this, the new distance between Jeanie and I. Separately, we each tried to explain; reassure them. I can't say for sure what she told them but as we all grew and their mother's health quickly worsened, it was clear who they blamed. To this day, twenty years after her death, it's a subject and time that's only referred to through their distance and absence; their mournful, unforgiving eyes.

Even that night, lying alone in the guest-room, it was Jeanie's allusions to Glenn and myself that unsettled me most. What she implied of our closeness — I could recognise aspects of truth. Began to look back in detail — still obsessively perhaps — to reassess all my feelings for Glenn. I had to recognise that he mesmerised me from that very first day; later, both as man and pianist, I found him magnetic. Without doubt he possessed a rare presence, and in his youthful days, before the medication bloated and ruined him, a striking physical beauty. Sometimes, hearing him play or simply watching him brood, deep in reflection, I would feel as if the air had been sucked from the room.

So was Jeanie right? Had I wanted more from our friendship? Did I recognise this and suppress it? If I had, for how long?

I was overtaken by guilt and anxiety. Even shied away from mass and communion, couldn't face Fr David beaming good wishes as we filed out of church. The thought of confession filled me with terror. Was there something I ought to confess? What was it exactly? For a while I envied Glenn his apparent agnosticism — for without faith's strictures where is anxiety, where's guilt? The only thing I recall him saying that pertained to an afterlife was a typical, tongue-in-cheek remark that touched on reincarnation.

'If I ever come back it'll be as some second-rate poet or media guru. I even dreamt of him lately . . . nice enough fellow, calls himself Caldwell, Sam Caldwell. Completely tone-deaf though, not a clue about music . . .'

Needless to say, though these doubts and reflections have spun through my head ever since, I never found the courage to raise them with Glenn. If not for my own peace of mind then for Jeanie's, I should have; but nothing approaching a suitable context arose. Now they are questions that will never be answered.

The truth is, I've played safe my whole life. Hid behind modest ambition, some form of status, how others see me. Convinced myself this was enough. *You're the most cautious man I know*, Jeanie once said. I laughed it off at the time, told her that was absurd. But who knew me better? Like Glenn, perhaps, I put things off for so long — plans, dreams, longings — that that's how they stayed. Why don't we act, speak up while we still have the chance? Eighty-odd years. For most, I fear, I've merely been sleepwalking.

When Lillian called me it was out of the blue.

'Is that Mr Seegers? Paul Seegers, the teacher?' Clearly not a young voice but still firm and commanding.

'Well, yes — ex-teacher,' I answered.

Strangely enough I'd been sorting through an old cabinet of Williamson papers when she rang. Consigning long-redundant folders and meeting notes to a collection of rubbish sacks on the floor of my study. Tim and Harriet wouldn't thank me for the task once I'd gone, so I'd gradually worked my way round the house, purging years of clobber.

'Oh, I'm so glad it's you,' she continued. 'Glenn spoke of you often, always with tremendous affection. Forgive me calling like this, my instinct was to write to you first but as I'll explain . . . My name is Lillian Getz, I don't know if you . . .'

As soon as she said it, of course, I knew who she was. *The Star* had printed the interview a year or so back. A respected sculptor in her eightieth year, living here in Toronto. Intended as a straightforward Arts section piece ahead of a major retrospective — since the feature appeared her work had become a side-issue while Lillian herself was suddenly of huge press interest, nationally and abroad. From the musical community especially. For during routine questions — about her youth, the artistic set she'd been part of — she'd revealed, almost as an aside, that she and Glenn had been lovers for close to four years, back in the late 1960s.

When I learnt of this my initial reaction was to dismiss her as a fantasist or worse; someone prepared to say anything for publicity. But having read and re-read the article as a whole, tried to match it with my own recollections of Glenn and that time, I could see that it might just be true.

To say I was stunned would seriously understate it. Up to then, despite our hiccoughs, I was certain that few had known Glenn better than I, or for longer. And from all I'd observed, he'd never shown much interest in girls or sex. (Florrie, I knew, had drummed into him early that both were beneath him, tawdry distractions from music, to be avoided at any cost). Even once we were adults, he never struck me as having the emotional maturity to sustain that kind of relationship. But if what this woman was saying was fact, then it undermined everything. My own judgement. How close Glenn and I really were — or could ever have been.

'Can I ask how you found me, Miss Getz? Just out of interest.' I sat down by the phone, scrabbling in the drawer for something to write with. I sensed I would need it.

'Lillian, please.' I could hear she was faintly amused by the question. 'Fortunately it wasn't so hard. You are the only Seegers in the directory.'

'Ah yes. That's true,' I said, feeling an idiot.

'I'm sorry, I can tell from your voice... but believe me, Paul — may I call you Paul? — I'd no plans to say what I did. To shock or hurt anyone. Or what a fuss this would cause. I'm an old woman, Glenn's been dead thirty years . . . I'm surprised there's still any interest. It's just that . . .' She paused. 'I suppose I've been sad a long time that no one knew the real truth about him. That if I took all this with me there'd be nothing but the same stupid stories for ever — how nutty and selfish he was, how alone. Some kind of hermit that didn't want or know love. And then I'd have done him a dreadful disservice. Because the Glenn that I knew was loving and kind and attentive...and, yes, a very passionate man.'

I was struggling for words, for an adequate response. It took me some moments.

'Yes, I understand your reasons. And I think it was brave of you. There's no denying it was something of a shock . . . I thought I knew most things about him. But I'm glad he found love. I am. No one could be unhappy at that.'

'Thank you. From all Glenn told me, I knew you were a generous man, Paul. A forgiving one, too.' I heard her sigh. 'To stay close to Glenn, a necessary quality, I'm sure you'll agree.'

We each reflected on that.

'Look, I know this is very presumptuous,' she went on, 'but there's something relating to him, something important I'd like to entrust you with. This afternoon, if that's at all possible. I'm not so far from you, I think . . .'

I wrote down her address then called a taxi to take me. (I didn't want to tell her—again pride forbade it—that though I still have my license I don't care for driving once winter approaches, especially after dark. It was early afternoon as I left but the sky was lowering already and I didn't know how long I'd be with her).

Not half-an-hour later I was speaking to the intercom outside her third-floor, downtown apartment. Admitted via a buzzer I found her seated in the small but immaculate living room, a tray of tea and biscuits already beside her. Examples of her work, small abstract pieces—most bronze or marble—were discreetly displayed round the room. There were shelves of books, many framed photos, several of Glenn.

'Please,' she lifted a hand from the rug on her lap to indicate the sofa. 'Come in, Paul—welcome. If you'd be kind enough to pour for us both . . . These hands are useless today.'

Straight-backed in an armchair she was slender and elegant, the shock of white hair swept back from her still striking face. It was a very odd feeling, I must say. To be suddenly in the home of a stranger, someone who'd known Glenn so intimately, whose existence I'd had not an inkling about through all of those years.

I sorted out the tea, set hers beside her. She lifted the

china cup carefully using both hands; took a sip. Most of her knuckles were swollen into spurs, two or three fingers effectively locked, curling into her palms. As I sat down she said:

'You're an intelligent man, Paul. You must have an idea why I asked you here?'

'Not really,' I replied honestly. 'I assume it's related to all the press interest. Beyond that . . .'

Driving over, my thoughts had turned once again to the period in question, my first years in charge at Williamson. Since the article was published I'd tried time and again to recall some detail, anything that with hindsight might confirm that Glenn was in love then, deeply engaged in a passionate romance. Surely there must have been signs? How could I not have suspected? My only defence is that states of manic excitement, exuberant passion—these were quite normal for Glenn. Had I or anyone else encountered him, on any given day, in this form of ecstatic mood we'd simply have attributed it to his latest musical enterprise. I wonder, now, if Glenn knew all along that he had this perfect emotional cover? Took conscious advantage. The only two times that I visited his St Clair apartment—one at least had been around then—there was certainly no hint of a feminine touch. Far from it. The floors were strewn with papers and books, LP covers, annotated scores, discarded sweaters and shoes. Wardrobes and bookcases covered most of the windows, blocking the daylight. It's hard to imagine any woman feeling comfortable there. Doubtless their assignations were mostly at Lillian's, or elsewhere.

'In a way, yes. Yes, it is.' If it were possible she sat up even straighter, fixed me with her clear grey eyes. 'I have a favour to ask of you, Paul. Please say no if you wish, I will understand. But as someone who knew and loved

Glenn as you did, someone he trusted—well, I know *I* can trust you.'

I nodded reflectively. The room was quiet save for the hiss of the gas fire, the gold carriage clock that ticked on the mantelpiece.

'It's not just the added attention,' she continued, 'though that's certainly unwelcome. Even now, on the rare occasions I get out at all, there's usually some fool with a camera. Or trying to ask further questions. As if there's any more to tell. The last one appeared at my hairdresser, can you believe? Seemed to know I was coming . . .

'The thing is, Paul, first it was just the arthritis, then I had to stop driving—now it's this. I can't do what I'd like anymore . . . one thing especially. I've always been to Glenn's grave on his birthday—until this year, at least. And on the date that he died.'

Only then did I realise. 'Oh my God, it's today.'

She nodded. 'And last year both visits were dreadful. Ruined by reporters who followed me there. I know it wasn't long since the piece came out, hopefully time has moved on, they'll have better things to do now. Either way, I can't go myself, not any more. And just in case there are still any halfwits . . .'

'Of course,' I assured her. 'It'll be an honour, Lillian. Just tell me what I can do . . .'

I make it back to the bench, slump heavily down, relieved to take the weight off my legs. My nose and lips are still numb but inside the coat I'm even perspiring a little, the deerstalker's flaps gently toasting my ears. And look, now it's starting to snow. Only lightly, in big soft flakes, but they settle, begin to whiten the ground at my feet.

I reach in again, locate the envelope. Lift it out, turn it over in my gloved hands. An hour or so ago I watched her scratch these two words upon it. *My Darling.* Slowly, with agonising care.

'Once you're there, Paul,' her eyes were bright and alert as she licked down the seal, held the envelope out to me, 'if you could read him the message . . . that would be nice.'

With some hesitation I open it up, ease something out. Not the card I expected. Something flimsier, older. A black and white photo, the image marked here and there, slightly faded. A small wooden cabin. Just beyond it, through trees, a fringe of water . . .

It's a long while ago, but I know the place instantly. Glenn's cottage next to Lake Simcoe. I bring the picture close to my eyes, try to pick out more detail. As the boughs around me stir, I swear I hear ripples lapping that shore. I'm breathing the piney, resinous scent of those woods in an instant. His retreat from it all. Somewhere he cherished, felt secure. His place to be alone, to practice and write. If Glenn brought you here you were lucky, there was no deeper sign of his trust. But that I knew only later. When first we were there, classmates together, idling whole days away, we knew nothing of luck or of what lay ahead. We'd dress up as pirates, push along the shallows in the family rowboat, Glenn's faithful mutt in the prow, barking at gulls . . .

I turn over the photo. On the reverse, covering each inch, is the same shaky script.

Hello, Bear,

Remember this? I know how you loved it. Me too. Nowhere

better, and no one more special to share it with. Who cares about time? — I live it as though it were yesterday. Thank you for taking me here, for letting me close. For everything, my darling.

So sorry I can't make it this time. Wherever you are, I'm there with you always, you know that. Just be patient, dear Bear, a little while longer. I'm coming.

Yours always.
L x x

Glancing around, there's no one in sight. I read it again, quietly but aloud, over Glenn's stone. When it's done I wedge the photo securely in the heart of the bouquet. Duty done, mission accomplished.

As I straighten this time my head spins. I don't know if it's faintness or continued bewilderment. I have to stand there a moment to steady myself.

Dusk has arrived and the three or four lamps down the path glow brighter with each passing second. Returning the photo to my pocket, I turn to head back, conscious that the cab still awaits me — and let out a gasp of surprise. The snow must have muffled his approach, for not ten yards away at the Gould memorial a tall broad-shouldered man, hatless but in a long heavy coat not unlike mine, is bending to peer at the inscription. As he leans forward I see from the side of his face that he's young, though his thin sandy hair is already receding.

As I move away carefully, back on to the path, he looks up. Gives a small friendly nod.

'Hello there,' I say, trying to sound jovial in response to his smile. 'If I stay any longer my toes will drop off! We must be real fans to be out here tonight . . .'

Stepping forward he takes his bare hands from his pockets, rubs them together in a similar gesture of empathy. 'Yes, sir. Absolutely.' The smile broadens. He seems genuinely pleased I have spoken. We face each other now, a couple of paces apart.

'You're a musician too? A pianist?'

'Hah, well . . . it hardly compares.' He shrugs self-consciously, flakes settling on his shoulders, in his hair. 'I'm studying at the Conservatory. Final year.' He holds out a hand. 'How do you do, sir. I'm Sam . . . Samuel Olsen.'

I shake automatically. What he's just said trips a wire. He must find my response very strange.

'Olsen?' I repeat. 'Not Caldwell?'

His brow furrows. I can see it in his eyes: he wants to help me but doesn't know how.

'Er . . . no. Not Caldwell, sir. My name is Sam Olsen.'

'Yes . . . yes, of course.' I'm still floundering. 'I'm so sorry, Sam . . . for a moment you reminded me of someone, that's all.' I introduced myself and said: 'Listen, if you and Glenn have the Conservatoire in common, that's a pretty good start. How about afterwards? Any plans?'

'Who knows?' The same shrug. 'I adore the Baroque—Bach, Mendelssohn, Reger. It was watching a documentary on Glenn that first got me into it. I mean, this guy could play! He was really sensational. I'm just a huge fan, sir—have all his recordings. And when I'm passing this way I try to stop by. You know it's the anniversary today? Twenty-six years since he died. Same year I was born, in fact.'

I nodded. 'It's why I'm here too.'

'Hey, that's really cool. Did you . . . did you know him?'

He seems genuinely awed at the prospect. But it's not a good time to ask me, and I have to get going. Even so, I'm surprised by my answer, it's speed. 'No,' I say, shaking my head. 'I can't say I did, not really.'

'Still, two fans together, huh?'

'He'll always have those, I'm certain of that. So, you heading this way?' I indicate the direction I'm going.

'No, I'm back over here,' he nods. So we shake hands again. 'Very good meeting you, sir . . . take care on these paths . . .'

He turns, moves off a few paces. Looks briefly back, raising a hand in farewell.

What a charming young man. Were there but more. Good manners, courtesy — respect for old lags like me — they may be small enough things, but without them I fear for the future sometimes.

The snow's really falling now, thicker and faster, swirling about us. As I'm watching him go he pulls something from his coat pocket, unfolds it, pulls it down tight on his head. And my heart skips a beat. It's a dark felt cap, a beret like Glenn's, exactly as he used to wear it. The fan's tribute. Black like his coat, dark as the broad and hunched shoulders trudging slowly away through the snowfall. For an instant I'm certain it *is* him. This is just as I pictured it, so many times down the years. When he spoke of the north with such rapture. His final withdrawal, his ultimate fugue.

The real music's out there, where silence and solitude are.

I stand and watch as the whiteness envelops him, takes him away from me, into the dream.